"Good Morning," Ridge Growled. "Did You Sleep Well?"

Dara smiled. "Like a baby."

Ridge scowled and turned away. "I'm glad one of us did."

Her heart tightened, but she made herself remain calm. "You're not going to give me one of those morning-after I-shouldn't-have-given-in-to-my-carnal-urges speeches, are you?"

Ridge sighed and met her gaze. "No. I couldn't regret last night, not one minute of it. But there are some things that last night can't change—that nothing can change."

"I wish you would tell me."

"No," he said firmly.

"Then tell me you're not going to pretend that we didn't make love. Or that you're just my bodyguard. Or that I'm just another client...."

Dear Reader,

Welcome to the wonderful world of Silhouette Desire! This month, look for six scintillating love stories. I know you're going to enjoy them all. First up is *The Beauty, the Beast and the Baby*, a fabulous MAN OF THE MONTH from Dixie Browning. It's also the second book in her TALL, DARK AND HANDSOME miniseries.

The exciting SONS AND LOVERS series also continues with Leanne Banks's *Ridge: The Avenger*. This is Leanne's first Silhouette Desire, but she certainly isn't new to writing romance.

This month, Desire has *Husband: Optional*, the next installment of Marie Ferrarella's THE BABY OF THE MONTH CLUB. Don't worry if you've missed earlier titles in this series, because this book "stands alone." And it's so charming and breezy you're sure to just love it!

The WEDDING BELLES series by Carole Buck is completed with *Zoe and the Best Man*. This series just keeps getting better and better, and Gabriel Flynn is one scrumptious hero.

Next is Kristin James' Desire, *The Last Groom on Earth*, a delicious opposites-attract story written with Kristin's trademark sensuality.

Rounding out the month is an amnesia story (one of my *favorite* story twists), *Just a Memory Away*, by award-winning author Helen R. Myers.

And *next* month, we're beginning CELEBRATION 1000, a very special, ultraspecial three-month promotion celebrating the publication of the 1000th Silhouette Desire. During April, May and June, look for books by some of your most beloved writers, including Mary Lynn Baxter, Annette Broadrick, Joan Johnston, Cait London, Ann Major and Diana Palmer, who is actually writing book #1000! These will be months to remember, filled with "keepers."

As always, I wish you the very best,

Lucia Macro
Senior Editor

Please address questions and book requests to:
Silhouette Reader Service
U.S.: 3010 Walden Ave., P.O. Box 1325, Buffalo, NY 14269
Canadian: P.O. Box 609, Fort Erie, Ont. L2A 5X3

LEANNE
BANKS
RIDGE: THE AVENGER

SILHOUETTE *Desire*®
Published by Silhouette Books
America's Publisher of Contemporary Romance

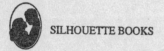

SILHOUETTE BOOKS

ISBN 0-373-05987-6

RIDGE: THE AVENGER

Books by Leanne Banks

Silhouette Desire

Ridge: The Avenger #987

Silhouette Special Edition

A Date With Dr. Frankenstein #983

*Sons and Lovers

LEANNE BANKS

is a national number-one bestselling author of romance. Recognized for her sensual writing with a Career Achievement Award from *Romantic Times* magazine, Leanne likes creating a story with a few grins, a generous kick of sensuality and characters that hang around after the book is finished. Leanne's favorite hobbies include hugging her children, dancing with her husband in the privacy of their home and going out to dinner...any night will do.

Acknowledgments to Commonwealth Confidential
Investigations and the Virginia Democratic
Headquarters. Special thanks to my incredibly
talented collaborators Cindy Gerard and
Susan Connell. And to the editor who pulled it all
together, what can I say? Lucia for president!

This book is dedicated to everyone who has ever held
a grudge, and experienced the power and
freedom of letting it go.

One

The irony of this situation was sweet.

So was Dara Seabrook's smile, Ridge Jackson thought as he observed the crowd of university students surrounding her. Presidential candidate Harrison Montgomery's goddaughter was seducing the younger vote with phenomenal success.

Her unswerving enthusiasm and optimism captured the demographic group that until recently had eluded Montgomery. Both the press and the camera were at her feet. In other words, Dara was pure gold. And like Fort Knox, she had to be protected.

College women admired her independent and intelligent image. And her hairstyle, Ridge added wryly, recalling that Dara's picture had recently appeared on the cover of a national newsmagazine.

Ridge knew the young studs weren't admiring her intelligence, however. They were getting lost in her intent blue-eyed gaze and wondering about the curve of her sweet smile. The more daring ones would skip the appeal of her face and concentrate on her body. A body, Ridge suspected, that would look a helluva lot better laid bare on a rumpled bed than wrapped in a classy but demure dress.

She turned, and beneath the brunette fringe of bangs on her forehead, he spotted the white bandage. That white bandage was the reason he was here. For the briefest moment Ridge wondered, as he always did at the beginning of a job, if protecting this person would cost his own life. In the next moment he dismissed the thought, and considered again the irony. He would protect Dara Seabrook with his life, and she would give him what he needed to make Harrison Montgomery pay.

Regional campaign coordinator Clarence Merriman fussed over Dara as they made their way to the limo. "You had no business coming out here today. You should have stayed in bed and rested. I don't know why I let you talk me into this. Your face looks like chalk."

Dara did feel woozy, but she would die before she admitted it. She deliberately misinterpreted his concern and kept walking, the heels of her black pumps sinking into the campus lawn. "Stop worrying. The picture they took for the paper will probably be in black and white, so no one will notice."

"*I'm* noticing," Clarence huffed indignantly. He made a tsking sound and put his hand at her elbow for support. "Your face looks like paste."

"Paste or chalk?" Dara smiled at the crotchety man she'd dubbed her baby-sitter. "Your declarations of my beauty are going to my head, but my stomach is complaining. Why don't we get a burger on the way to the hotel? Then you can tuck me into my room, and I can get out of these clothes, and—"

Dara's voice trailed off as her gaze collided with a tall stranger studying her as he stood beside the limo. With unusual golden brown eyes, he gave her a once-over that seemed to catalog her height, weight and birthmarks within a matter of seconds.

His navy suit didn't conceal the impressive breadth of his shoulders, his dark hair touched the edge of his collar, and she might have been fooled into believing he was just another handsome man if she had missed the determined set of his jaw.

He gave the impression of masculine power, not the fake-it-till-you-make-it kind she observed in many of the political hopefuls she met every day. This had more to do with a personal power than with the make of a man's suit or who his daddy was. She admired the rare quality at the same time she felt intimidated by it.

She was accustomed to being watched, but not with this level of intensity. Uncomfortable, she looked at Clarence. He was fumbling through his notebook.

"Oh, I almost forgot," Clarence said as the autumn breeze fluttered the pages. "You must be Mr. Jackson with...with—" Clarence frowned at his notes.

"Sterling Security," the man finished in a voice that managed to mix steel and velvet, and turned his gaze back to Dara. "I'm here for Miss Seabrook."

Dara's stomach took a dive.

He pulled out his ID for Clarence and her to glance at, then opened the limo door. "I understand she has a busy schedule this evening, so I thought we could brief each other on the way to the hotel."

Looking everywhere but at Dara, Clarence cleared his throat. "Well, of course."

It finally dawned on Dara that she'd just been assigned another baby-sitter, one she was quite sure she didn't want. "Just one minute." She glared at Clarence. "I thought we discussed this last night," she began. "I thought—"

"It's out of Mr. Merriman's hands, Miss Seabrook. Mr. Montgomery arranged for my services."

Clarence shot her a look of apology and shrugged help-lessly. "I'll sit in the front while you two fill each other in."

"Fill each other in on what?" Dara's head was begin-ning to pound. She stared mutinously at the security man and crossed her arms over her chest. If truth were told, all the campaign publicity was beginning to wear on her. She had four more weeks of heavy exposure to the public eye, and it would take all her resources to tamp down her growing impatience with the press's superficial obsession with her hairstyle, clothing, and manicure. She felt lonely and a little disconnected. A bodyguard at her elbow every minute would likely send her straight over the edge. "Your presence really isn't necessary," she said crisply, because she suspected a diplomatic approach wouldn't work with this man.

Mr. Jackson lifted an eyebrow. "What about the beer bottle one of Montgomery's detractors threw at you?"

Dara resisted the urge to touch the bandage and waved her hand in a dismissive gesture. "It was a random inci-dent. A few stitches," she fudged.

"It's my job to make that kind of random incident nonexistent, and I understand it was fifteen stitches."

Dara chafed at the invasion to her privacy. Someone at campaign headquarters had probably filled this stranger in on all the details about the "incident." She shook her head. "This is silly. I'm not in any danger. I don't need a bodyguard."

There wasn't an ounce of give in his stance, but she thought she saw the faintest sliver of understanding pass through his eyes. "It's out of your hands."

Frustration rolled through her, but she knew she couldn't cause a scene. She'd learned the press was every-where. Dara got into the car, dropped her head back against the leather upholstery, and resolved to call her godfather as soon as she got back to her room. Feeling the man sit across from her as the limo pulled forward, she closed her eyes to block out his presence, but it didn't work. "I didn't get a good look at that ID you flashed. You're not connected with the Secret Service, are you, Mr. Jackson?" she finally asked after a few moments' silence.

"No. Since you're technically not a member of Mr. Montgomery's family, you're not covered under government protection." He pressed his ID into her hand. "Call me Ridge."

Dara's eyes popped open. She didn't want to call him anything. "I'm not going to know you long enough to call you Ridge."

The leather holder was warm from the heat of his body, and his gaze said he knew she was trying to ignore him. And not succeeding. She appraised him again. He was big enough to be threatening, but lean enough to be able to move fast. She wouldn't want to meet him in an alley.

"We'll see." Ridge glanced out the window and narrowed his eyes. "This wasn't the planned route I discussed with the chauffeur."

Dara spotted the familiar sight of golden arches and felt an impertinent dart of joy. "Clarence is trying to appease me with comfort food." The limo pulled into the take-out lane for the fast-food restaurant. Her sense of humor resurfaced, and she smiled broadly. "What do you want on your hamburger?"

Back at her hotel suite, Dara's eyes glazed over at the list of rules, directions, and precautions Ridge Jackson delivered during the next hour. Her reactions ranged from mild disinterest, to impatience, to an overwhelming urge to tell the man to *chill out*. She was just about to give in to that urge when sudden, blissful silence filled the room.

"You haven't listened to a word I've said." Ridge tried, but failed to keep the impatience from his voice. It amazed him that such a charming woman could elicit such exasperation.

Dara shook her head and stood. "Oh, no. I heard the first fifteen minutes. After that, I was sure I'd been brought to some sort of Nazi torture room, so I started fantasizing about the sixty-minute bath I'd planned to take. At the moment, the only thing I want is to get rid of my campaign clothes, sink into a hot tub, and let my bath oil take me away."

The picture she drew with her voice taunted his imagination. It was easy to envision Dara Seabrook naked and wet. During the last thirty minutes she'd slipped off her leather shoes and shimmied out of her jacket, all the while nibbling on the straw of her diet cola. Her lipstick was gone, and Ridge couldn't decide which way her mouth looked better: lined with a provocative red lipstick, or just plain bare. He brushed aside the thought. "You can have your bath in a few minutes. We need to work out a special password for—"

"Later." She met his gaze. "Due to your discourse, my sixty-minute bath has been reduced to fifteen." She stepped closer to him. "I'm still not convinced you're staying. But just in case you are, you've given me all your rules and regulations. Now here's one of mine, Mr. Jackson. *Don't mess with my bath.*"

With that, Ridge was treated to the sight of Dara's shapely derriere just before she walked into her bedroom and firmly shut the door.

"I don't like him," Dara said to her godfather, Harrison Montgomery, as she soaked in the tub.

Harrison's muffled laughter carried through the phone wire. "I don't believe you. You like everybody."

"I don't need a bodyguard." Dara deepened her voice and imitated a well-known senator. "You know it, I know it, and the American people know it."

Harrison laughed again shortly, then grew quiet. "I want you to humor me on this. You know how Helen and

I feel about you. You're the daughter we never had. If anything happened to you while you're campaigning for me, I'd never forgive myself."

Hearing the sincere concern in his voice, Dara sighed. She'd spent so much time reassuring everyone else about the incident that she hadn't dealt with her own feelings. She *had* been frightened, but heaven forbid that she should tell anyone else that. "It was just a few stitches."

"And this is just for four weeks," he countered. "You can handle anything for four weeks. Then you can take off for some sunny island and forget about politics and bodyguards."

Dara felt the gentle persuasive pressure in his voice and she knew she was stuck with a bodyguard. "Does it have to be him?"

"Has he been rude?" Harrison's tone immediately cooled.

Dara rolled her eyes at the ceiling. "No, but, couldn't you have gotten someone more..." She groped for an adequate description and found all her choices were ridiculous. "Maybe I mean less..."

"Less what?"

Less confident? Less domineering? Less sexy?

Dara kicked at her dissolving bubbles in frustration. "Someone more like Clarence?"

Harrison chuckled. "Clarence wouldn't hurt a flea. You've got the best man for the job. I checked around, and Sterling Security's reputation is formidable. I spoke to the head of the agency and told him to send his best bodyguard."

Subject closed. Dara heard the door shut on the subject. As she and Harrison concluded their conversation with a few pleasantries, she felt the ominous knowledge down to her bones.

She was stuck with Ridge.

* * *

Ridge watched Dara step through the door and felt her blue-eyed gaze immediately latch onto his. *Grudging acceptance, but no surrender,* her face said. She wasn't exactly what he'd expected. Underneath all that demure, sweet charm was a kick that would likely land another man on his butt.

The scent and sight of her bombarded his senses. Ridge felt like he was under full frontal assault. Her dark hair was piled loosely on her head, with her fringe of bangs and tendrils framing her face. She smelled like a dark, secret passion and looked like trouble waiting to happen. Her black cocktail dress faithfully and devotedly followed every curve of her body with the same fervor a Boy Scout made a promise.

Ridge, however, had never been a Boy Scout.

Her gaze swept over him as if she were checking his appearance. The moment lasted just a shade too long for his pride, so he called her on it. "Everything look okay? Or do you need a closer look?"

Her lashes lowered, momentarily hiding her eyes from him. "My vision is just fine from here. I'm sure you've had more than enough women tell you that you look better than fine." She glanced up then. "But that's not the issue, is it? I talked to Harrison, and he insists you're the best."

Ridge felt a strange twinge at Montgomery's acknowledgment of his abilities.

When he remained silent, she sighed. "He also insists that you remain my bodyguard."

"If you hate the idea of having a bodyguard so much, why don't you remove the risk and stop campaigning?"

Dara shook her head. "That's not an option. I owe Harrison. I'm not sure it's the kind of debt that can ever be paid in full, but I can help him now, in this role." She shrugged. "Besides, I believe in him. If ever a man was born and bred to be president, it's Harrison Montgomery."

At her words, a deep resentment burned in his gut. He knew Montgomery had been raised in a privileged home by two supportive parents, had attended the best schools, and married a wife with a pedigree. On the other hand, Ridge had been raised in near poverty by a drug-addicted single mother and he had barely graduated from public high school. With the help of the United States Marine Corps, however, he'd worked past his anger and made something of himself. Dara's blind admiration brought every cynical instinct to the surface. "I suppose you agree with all his views."

Dara paused and looked at him curiously. "No. I wouldn't say I agree with *all* his views. But I do think he'll make a great leader for our country. My opinion may be partly influenced by my personal experience with him. Harrison has been a stable, supportive force in my life since I was born." Something dark and painful flickered in her eyes, and her voice softened. "Sometimes, he was the only stable, supportive person."

He wondered at the source of the pain in her gaze, but she cleared her throat and smiled self-consciously. "That's another story, though. One you're probably not interested in, so—"

"Don't bank on it," Ridge interjected.

"Bank on what?"

"Don't assume that I'm not interested in hearing anything about you."

Dara felt the strangest clutch of excitement in her chest. His direct gaze left her floundering. "I, uh, I—" She cursed her stammering tongue. Heaven help her, she'd been coached by one of the best media specialists in the country to deliver a stutter-free speech. Why was she fumbling now?

"Knowing you is part of my job, and as Montgomery told you, I do my job very well."

Dara blinked. He wasn't interested in her personally, she realized. He was only interested in her professionally. Humiliation flooded her chest. Anger followed soon after. Why should she care what Ridge Jackson thought of her? He was just an overgrown baby-sitter.

She took a deep breath to calm herself. "I'm sure you've been given all the information you need to do your job." She fought the edge she felt creeping into her voice. "We really need to be leaving for the dinner with the Chamber of Commerce. I've already phoned my escort—" Unable to recall the man's name, she frowned and reached for her calendar in her purse. "Tom," she said finally, feeling Ridge's eyes on her and wondering why he made her feel more nervous than when she stood in front of a crowd of thousands. "Tom Andrews. I told him we'd pick him up on the way. Is that okay?"

"Fine. Do you need your coat?"

"Yes." She reached for the blue wool cape, but Ridge put it around her shoulders.

"You know you're safe with me, don't you, Dara?"

"Of course," she murmured, but something about his velvet-and-steel voice didn't make her feel the least bit *safe*.

Ridge watched the crowd, not Dara. That was his job, after all. Still, he was aware of her every move. While he watched the exits, he heard her give Harrison Montgomery a glowing recommendation. His gaze moving constantly over the crowd, he wondered how she had managed to rouse the conservative group to wild applause after her brief speech. If she was Montgomery's secret weapon, then she was more effective than the Pied Piper. He could just hear the sounds of levers being pulled on the voting machines, all for Montgomery.

It was enough to make him puke.

Ridge kept his seething temper to himself, as he had for fourteen years. The perfect moment would come, he knew it in his bones, when he could take his vengeance against Montgomery. This consuming grudge Ridge held against the presidential candidate had the potential to destroy him, and the time had come to do something about it.

He had a plan to settle the score. The first step was gaining Montgomery's trust. If Ridge had wanted to exact his revenge from a distance he could have called one of the rag magazines and spilled his story, but it wasn't enough just to ruin him. He wanted Montgomery to hurt, to feel a fraction of the betrayal Ridge had felt when he watched his mother die. Maybe then, he could rid himself of the anger that had burned inside him for so long. Maybe then, he could find peace.

Mindful of the woman who would unknowingly help him accomplish his goal, Ridge looked at Dara and saw her check her watch. When she thought no one was looking, she squeezed the bridge of her nose and closed her eyes. Opening them, she glanced in his direction and nodded. That was the prearranged signal for them to leave. Ridge motioned the chauffeur to collect the limo while Dara said her goodbyes.

"It's been lovely," she said to the mayor. "I appreciate your including me tonight, and I'll be sure to pass on your good wishes to Harrison."

Her escort stood beside her. "Let me walk you to the car. Are you sure you don't want to go out for a drink? There's a nice lounge just around the corner." He placed his hand at her back. "Or if you want to get away from the crowd, we could go to my place."

Dara shook her head and smiled, flashing her dimple. "I'd love to, but it's been a long day. Maybe—"

Tom Andrews turned on the charm. "Aw, come on, just one little drink. I get introduced to a beautiful woman only to have to tell her goodbye three hours later."

Walking behind the couple, Ridge decided he couldn't fault the guy for his persistence. He could fault him for other reasons, though. Ridge would bet that Dara's date was hoping to use her to pump up his own political prospects. Andrews was running for the state senate.

Dara pulled slightly away and folded her hands. "I've enjoyed meeting you, too," Ridge heard her say. "But my schedule is just crazy for the next four weeks. Maybe after the election," she said vaguely.

"Thirty minutes, just thirty minutes so we can get to know each other better," Tom said in a voice Ridge thought was ten percent desperation, twenty percent seduction, and seventy percent slime.

Either Tom was being deliberately obtuse, or he had the sensitivity of an alligator. Ridge withheld a sigh. There was no way he'd let Dara alone with that guy. They still hadn't worked out a password. He stepped forward and pointed toward the front door. "The limo's here, Dara. Remember, you have an early start tomorrow."

Dara glanced at Ridge in confusion. "Actually, I was planning to sleep—"

"And the doctor said to make sure you got your rest," he interrupted. "I'm sure you understand," he said to Tom as he ushered her toward the car.

"You've got my card," Tom called to Dara. "Give me a call."

"Thank you again, Tom." She shot Ridge a look of disapproval as he tried to stuff her into the limo. "Will you wait one minute? I don't want to be rude."

"It's part of my job to cut down on your exposure time," Ridge explained. "We're on a public street."

Dara rolled her eyes and slid into the car. When Ridge started to close her door, she shook her head and crooked her finger. "I believe we need to talk."

As soon as he joined her, she turned to him. "Don't do that again. I won't have you acting like some overgrown nanny. I had no intention of extending the evening with Tom, but you have no rights over my private life.''

"It's my job to protect you no matter who you're with," Ridge corrected, and could see she was gearing up for a fight.

"And what if I want to go out for a date? Just where do you draw the line, Ridge? Is it part of your job to come into my bedroom, too?"

He narrowed his eyes at that last remark. At another time, *in another life,* he corrected himself, her insinuation might have prompted a full range of responses, some more satisfying than others. If he were in Dara Seabrook's bedroom, he sure as hell wouldn't just be watching her. Ridge ruthlessly stuck to the facts. "According to your file, since you've been campaigning, you haven't begun a romantic relationship or brought a man back to your room to stay the night. Your file—"

Dara's indignant gasp was more effective than a scream. "My file!" Even in the dim light of the limo, he could see the color in her cheeks deepen. "Who in hell gave you that kind of private information about me? Who—"

"It's standard procedure." Ridge kept his voice neutral, recalling that the file had also said Dara cursed only when extremely upset. "The information is gathered so I don't walk in cold wondering what your habits are." She looked like she wanted to hit him, and Ridge couldn't decide if he was irritated or amused. "If you want to see it, I'll show it to you."

"You're damn right I want to see it, but that's just the beginning." Her gaze met his, and Ridge felt the punch of her feminine determination clear down to his bones. "If I've got to be with you day-in and day-out for the next four weeks, I want to see your file, too."

Two

For a second, Dara wondered if she'd gone too far. The little sensation unfurling in her stomach told her she had.

Ridge stared at her with both masculine challenge and pity for her heated demands. Leaning back in the seat opposite her, he unbuttoned his suit jacket so that it slid back to reveal the stark contrast of his black leather holster and gun against his white shirt. It was enough of a mix of civilized and uncivilized to make her uneasy. His dark trousers stretched taut against muscular thighs spread wide in a typically male pose that somehow made her think of him in anything but a typical way.

"Tell me what you want to know," he said in that velvet-and-steel voice she was becoming more and more familiar with.

She could imagine him using that same tone with a lover. Only then he would say, "Tell me what you want, baby." Her stomach tightened.

Dara scolded herself for her outrageous thoughts. Playing with a man like Ridge would just get a woman like her burned. If she were prudent, she'd say forget it and fold her hand of cards with this little skirmish. More than her feminine pride, however, was on the line. She sensed that any shred of autonomy she could maintain during the next four weeks hung in the balance. Pushing back fear and another more vague emotion, Dara straightened in her seat. "Age," she said crisply.

He lifted an eyebrow. "Thirty."

"How long were you in the service?"

"How do you know I was in the service?"

She shrugged, gaining back her equilibrium. "Your manner, the way you walk." She glanced at his feet then back to his face and smiled slightly. "Your well-shined shoes."

"Ten years, a marine."

She nodded. "I guess that means you've been a bodyguard for—"

"Two years as a civilian. I worked on special assignment in that capacity for four years when I was a marine."

Dara hesitated only a second. Her natural impulse was to respect another person's privacy. "Family?"

His gaze turned cool. "None. My mother and grandparents are dead."

No wife. No mother. No children. *No business of hers.* "You don't like answering questions about yourself, do you?"

"I've learned that you have to reach a meeting of the minds with your clients. It makes the job work more smoothly." He glanced away. "Most clients aren't interested in me, though. They just want me to do my job."

Dara pictured Ridge's usual client—a businessman, perhaps a rock musician, someone from a foreign country. They probably all treated him like he was part of the woodwork. She laughed at the ridiculous notion.

He looked at her curiously.

"I guess I'm not like most of your clients, am I?"

His gaze skimmed over her. "No."

Lord, he was stingy with his answers. She sighed. "What else do you know about me?"

He cocked his head to one side. "The regular stats. You graduated with a Liberal Arts degree three years ago and went to work for Montgomery. I've been briefed on your close contacts and some of your habits—you don't last much past midnight if you've gone full-speed all day. You're not usually demanding, but you prefer to feel like you have some say over your situation. I'll have to agree with that one," he said, his voice dry.

"And if you were in this situation, would you be any different?"

"No," he admitted, but he looked as if he would like to argue the point. He loosened his tie. "The file said you have a lot of friends, but you've put those relationships on the back burner because of the election. You stay in touch with your mother. You've been out with a dozen men in the last several months on outings while you campaign for your godfather, and you've politely turned them all down when they asked for another date."

"And you really wonder why?" she asked. Thus far, Ridge had been incredibly perceptive. She was surprised he hadn't figured out her reasons on his own.

Ridge shrugged. "The only lethal thing about that guy tonight was his line."

Dara laughed and shook her head. "Oh, I don't think so."

"Right," he said, his voice full of skepticism.

"I get this all the time. I'm given an escort to most of these functions. It's part of the job, but these men are all the same. They all want the same thing—and it's not my heart, not my soul. Or my body.''

Ridge's gaze flicked over her, lingering on her legs, as if he seriously doubted that last statement.

Dara smoothed her hand over the hem of her dress. "They all want a closer connection with Harrison, and they're hoping they can get it through me."

Understanding flickered across his face. "And you want?"

Dara hesitated, wondering how the conversation had meandered back to such a personal topic. "Wasn't that in my file?"

He held her gaze, shaking his head slowly.

Fighting an urge to fidget she thought she'd conquered years ago, Dara sighed. She still felt a pinch when she remembered how she'd fallen hard for one man's line, only to learn that what he'd really wanted was an association with her godfather. The experience had made her gun-shy. "It sounds corny," she said quietly, "but I just want to be wanted for me. I want someone who, for the most part, doesn't really care that I'm Harrison Montgomery's goddaughter."

Dara resisted her need to look away from Ridge although she was too aware of him, of how close his knee was to hers, of how his musky male scent mingled with her perfume, of how curious she was about him when she shouldn't be. Taking a deep breath, she instinctively turned the conversation away from herself. "And what about you? What do you want?"

A charged silence stretched and tightened between them. Ridge leaned forward and placed his hands on either side of her legs. His teeth flashed in a slow, big-bad-wolf grin. "Are you making an offer, Miss Seabrook?"

Her heart hammered against her rib cage. Heat and confusion tangled inside her. "I, uh, I—"

"Because if you are..."

Panic won over excitement. "No!" She pressed her back against the seat. "I was just wondering—"

"I'm wondering, too," Ridge interrupted in a voice threaded with intimacy. "I'm wondering what's going on in your mind when your eyelids flutter."

Her mouth desert dry, she stared at him.

He slid his thumb just under the hem of her dress on the outside of her thigh and her breath hitched in her throat. Watching her with his compelling, golden eyes, he moved his thumb in one slow stroke that made her feel branded. "I wonder a lot more, but if you're concerned that I'll take advantage of you, don't worry. It's my job to guard your body, Dara, and that's what I'll do, even if it means protecting you from me." Ridge removed his hands and eased away from her. "I make it a policy never to get involved with a client."

Heaven help her if he changed his mind! She'd been about as threatening as a wet noodle. She should have slapped his inquisitive hands. Next time she would. This time, she just wanted an ice cube. Dara searched for her breath and finally found it. "Good," she managed to say, nodding emphatically and wishing her hands would stop trembling. "Very good. I think that sounds like a... uh—" She cleared her throat and wondered why she felt like a bomb had gone off inside her. "A wise policy," she finished, and breathed a sigh of relief when the limo pulled to a stop outside the hotel.

"Here they are. Just what you ordered." Wearing a dubious expression, Clarence handed the bag to Dara.

Sitting on the plush sofa of her hotel suite, Dara glanced inside the bag and gave a weak smile. "Thank you. They look fine. Did you find anyone who can coach me?"

Clarence adjusted his bow tie. "I asked a couple of people at the local campaign headquarters, discreetly of course, but none of them had any, uh, experience with, uh, rollerblades.''

Ridge watched the interplay between the two of them curiously.

Dara sighed and tucked a lock of her damp hair behind her ear. Fresh from a morning shower, wearing blue jeans that cupped her well-shaped rear end and revealed tantalizing hints of bare flesh from strategically placed tears, along with a Mickey Mouse T-shirt that stretched across her breasts, she looked more like a college coed than the current darling of the press. Her face and feet were bare. With all the polish rubbed off of her, she still exuded a subtle but provocative energy that lured his attention and held it.

The only thing that proved, he told himself, was that his hormones were in working order.

"I don't want to sound vain," she said, "but this is something I really don't want to see on the evening news for the rest of my natural life."

Clarence nodded sympathetically. "Forrester should have asked you first, but you know how he is when he gets going. I suppose we could attempt to cancel," he said, his voice full of doubt.

"It would be easier to die."

Ridge tried to put the pieces of the conversation together. He knew Drew Forrester was Montgomery's crackerjack media specialist. "Cancel what?" he finally interjected.

Both heads turned toward him. Reservation shimmered in Dara's eyes. She'd deliberately ignored him since last night. Ridge wondered if that was a result of his actions, and felt the slightest sting of regret. He'd intentionally made her uncomfortable because he'd seen that reckless glint in her eyes, the womanly curiosity. Perhaps he could have let it pass if he hadn't felt an answering flicker of restlessness inside him. But, *hell*, the last thing he needed was for Montgomery's goddaughter to spin her feminine wiles around his head and seduce him.

"Cancel what?" he repeated.

Clarence cleared his throat. "Well, it seems that Mr. Forrester accepted an invitation for Miss Seabrook to participate in an athletic event for the purpose of promoting Mr. Montgomery's campaign."

Dara threw Clarence a long-suffering glance. "What Clarence means is that Drew promised the three major television networks and the rest of the free world that I would skate in a parade next week." She pulled the pair of hot pink and black in-line skates from the bag and spun one of the wheels. "I'm surprised this wasn't in my file, too," she muttered darkly under her breath, then tossed Ridge a look of defiance. "I can't skate, can't ski, can barely dance. It took me a long time to get used to high heels."

Her confession amused him, but he restrained himself from laughing. "And you can't cancel," he said, confirming her earlier statement.

"Drew doesn't understand the meaning of the word 'no,'" she said glumly.

"Quite true," Clarence agreed. He paused, assessing Ridge. "I don't suppose you know how to—"

"Absolutely not," Dara said, rising from the sofa. "It's not in Mr. Jackson's job description to teach me how to skate. Besides, I'm sure he hasn't spent the last few years whizzing around on in-line skates, so—"

"I could teach you," Ridge casually intoned. "I've been on rollerblades a few times. And a fair portion of my misspent youth," he added cynically, "was spent on skateboards." There'd been so much darkness when he was a teenager, that sometimes all he could recall of that time was his mother and her addictions. He was surprised by the faint glimmer of his fond memory. "I even won a ribbon once."

"That doesn't mean—" Dara began.

"What size skates do you wear?" Clarence asked.

"Eleven."

Clarence was already on his way out the door when Dara called after him. "Clarence!" She ran to the door. "Wait! I don't want—" She groaned in exasperation when the door closed behind the campaign coordinator. "Oh, Lord, save me from controlling men." She turned around to face Ridge. "You really don't know what you're getting into. You may carry a gun and know how to go hand-to-hand with the bad guys, but you are really out of your league on this one. This is going to take more than patience."

Ridge had to confess that Dara was turning this into the most interesting job he'd had in years. "I'm a patient man," he said in a mild voice.

She waved her hand dismissively. "This is going to take more than skill."

"I have plenty of skill."

"You don't understand. This is going to take a miracle. We are talking about a woman who gets dizzy walking across the beginner's balance beam. I never could balance a book on my head for my finishing school class. I'm not a balanced kind of person."

Complete silence followed. Ridge cleared his throat to cover the chuckle he couldn't contain.

Dara narrowed her eyes. "I didn't mean that the way it sounded."

"I'm sure you didn't," Ridge agreed, but couldn't keep his amusement from his voice.

"I meant that I have a problem with keeping my balance."

"Right."

Dara gave him a withering glance. "If I hear you make one crack about my being unbalanced, I'll—" Tossing her head, she glared at him, obviously trying to come up with a suitable threat. "I don't know what I'll do, but I'll do something rash," she promised, all heat and bluster.

Something rash. Ridge irreverently wondered what that would be. He'd love to see it. "I haven't said a word."

"Yes, you have," she muttered. "You just didn't say it out loud."

Three hours later, in a quiet little park, Dara's rear end came into intimate contact with concrete for the twentieth time. "That's it!" She began tugging at the laces to her skates. "I won't be able to sit down for a whole week."

"You're quitting."

Dara heard the surprise in Ridge's voice and glanced at him. "I wish. No. This is just a temporary retreat. I'll try again in a couple of days." She turned her attention back to the laces and felt her own jolt of surprise when Ridge's strong, warm hand covered hers.

"One last try," he said, leaning down beside her. "This time I'll pull you."

Dara had rejected this suggestion every time he'd made it. She could handle the instructions, and though he hadn't made any jokes, she could have handled them, too. She just didn't want him touching her. He made her feel flustered. "We've been over this. You won't be able to pull me in the parade. I need to be able to do it myself."

"And you will. This is just one of the steps in learning. C'mon." He gently urged her to her feet.

Immediately feeling her feet roll in opposite directions, she grasped for Ridge. "I'm going to fall again," she said, half warning, half plea. "I'm going to—"

Ridge pulled her flush against the front of him. "No, you're not," he growled, his voice full of determination, his body a wall of rock-solid strength.

Struggling for a sense of balance that was depressingly elusive, she looked up at him and shook her head. "You're taking this personally and you really shouldn't. I warned you it would take a miracle. I told you—"

Ridge's hard gaze met hers and Dara bit her tongue. "You *will* learn to skate. I'll make sure of it."

She had a sinking feeling in the pit of her stomach. "Have you always been this strong-willed?"

Something flickered in his eyes, perhaps a memory, Dara thought, because his expression relaxed slightly.

"Yeah, I guess I have," he said. "What about you?"

She was surprised by his assessment. Most people didn't remark on her will. For the most part, Dara thought she kept that quality well hidden. She glanced down. "No. As a matter of fact, I haven't."

"Make your skates face forward," he told her. "And hold on."

"Don't worry," she murmured, concentrating on her feet.

"Look up. If you watch your feet, you'll end up tripping. You have to watch where you're going."

He started skating backward, pulling her gently along. "So when did you develop your stubbornness?"

"I thought we used the term strong-willed." Keeping her gaze trained over Ridge's right shoulder, Dara tried not to think about the warm, bulging biceps she was clinging to, the way Ridge's hands curled around her waist, and the brush of his spearmint-scented breath over her face as he chuckled.

"Okay," he conceded. "Strong-willed."

Their speed picked up the slightest bit and Dara tightened her grasp. "My mother raised me, and she was sick a lot when I was growing up. I guess you could say it was a case of what doesn't destroy us makes us stronger." She felt his gaze on her and looked up at him to find him regarding her intently. "What?"

He paused. "My mother was sick a lot, too."

She felt a wave of understanding and saw the same emotion mirrored on his face. In that one moment there was a link between them, a shared experience that had shaped and hurt and left its imprint.

In some corner of her mind she heard a bird chirping and felt the October breeze brush over her, but her senses were dominated by the man who held her in his arms. As she clung to him, she sensed they'd both stepped onto a tiny piece of common ground, and for the first time in months she didn't feel alone. "How long was she sick?"

Ridge slowed, and the distance between their bodies dwindled from inches to centimeters. "From the time I was born until the day she died. She was a drug addict."

She heard the grief, and again, identified with it. His gaze flickered between her eyes and mouth, and Dara held her breath. His eyes were tawny, nearly topaz. She'd always thought of them as unusual, and now she knew why. They reminded her of a lion's eyes, compelling and a bit untamed. A ripple of awareness quivered and quaked inside her.

His closeness was an emotional and sensual seduction more powerful than anything she'd ever experienced. It scraped off the layer of poise she'd hidden behind for months, leaving her bare. His chest was no more than a breath away from her breasts. Her heart pounded, and she didn't know if she should stop the spell or make it last. But another need surfaced, the need to be known.

"My mother is mentally ill," Dara confided quietly. "She wasn't diagnosed for a long time. When she stays on her medication, she does well, but sometimes she forgets." She took a deep breath. "I always thought it would have been nice to have my dad around, but he wasn't." She shrugged, suddenly wondering if she'd revealed too much. "What about your father?"

Ridge's gaze turned turbulent. "He wasn't in the picture, either."

"My father died. He—"

"Mine might as well have," Ridge said, his tone flat, his eyes giving away the anger.

Dara sensed an immediate distancing from him, and felt upset. It was as if he had teased her by opening the door a crack, then slamming it quickly. Stiffening in distress, she looked down and immediately stumbled, the movement throwing her against Ridge's chest again. "Oh! I'm sorry. I think—"

"You looked down again," Ridge said in a low voice that made her too aware of how close his mouth was to her forehead.

Desperately struggling for her equilibrium, she shook her head. "I know, I know. It's a terrible habit, isn't it? I think the lesson has lasted long enough." She pushed ineffectually at his chest. "This sidewalk's done enough damage to my rear—"

Ridge swore. "Stop pushing me away. You'll fall again."

Falling was okay, Dara thought. Falling was easier than being held by Ridge. "Then I'll just sit down so I can get out of these skates," she announced, immediately bending her knees.

"Let me help—" Ridge began to kneel.

"No!"

Ridge stared at her.

Dara winced. She lowered her voice and managed a small smile, but she didn't even attempt looking at him. "I appreciate it, but I can do this much myself. Really," she insisted when he sat beside her. "You've done too much."

Dara meant that last statement with all of her heart. In more ways than one, and in every way that counted, Ridge had done entirely too much.

After they left the park Ridge gave Dara a wide berth, as much for himself as for her. Quiet and guarded, she kept her conversation with him to a minimum. It was so different from the openness she'd exhibited that he felt a strange sense of loss. He wasn't totally sure what had happened back there, but he knew it shouldn't happen again. There was one thing he was sure of, though.

He had wanted to kiss her.

Not just a gentle, friendly brushing of their lips. What he'd really wanted was to taste her, to slide past her lips and teeth and take her breath and let her take his. He'd wanted the tangle of her sweet tongue with his. And if he were honest, he would admit that he wanted to join more than his mouth with Dara.

Stifling an oath, Ridge decided honesty was definitely overrated. He needed Dara for one thing, and it wasn't sex. He needed her to get to Montgomery.

When they returned to the hotel suite, Dara flipped through her messages and frowned. "I've got some calls to make. My mother and Drew," Dara said, looking worried. She headed for her bedroom.

The expression on her face gnawed at him. "Is she okay?"

Dara glanced over her shoulder, meeting his gaze for the first time since they'd left the park. Caution and need smoldered in the blue depths of her eyes. Ridge wondered how he'd ever thought of her as cool and superficial. "I don't know," she said, and hesitated for a moment. Then her lashes swept down, shuttering her eyes from him. "Thanks for asking."

Two hours later, after Ridge had heard the faint lilt of her voice beyond the wall and the rush of water for her bath, Dara came back into the darkened living room of the suite where he sat watching a ballgame on TV. Dara gave a covetous glance to the two slices of pizza left in the box.

"You can have it," Ridge offered.

"Are you sure?" Standing in front of the coffee table, she paused, wondering if she should have just stayed in her room the rest of the night. She could have waited until tomorrow to tell Ridge about the change in schedule, but she'd felt restless and hungry.

"I'm sure." Rising, he took a few steps into the adjoining kitchenette and opened the refrigerator. "Beer or cola?"

Dara nudged the olives off a piece of pizza and took a bite. "I don't suppose there's a margarita or two in there."

Ridge cracked a smile at the wistfulness in her voice. "No, but I'm sure we could get one sent up from the bar."

"Any Mrs. Fields chocolate-chip cookies?"

Ridge lifted an eyebrow. "Is this a list of Dara Seabrook's favorite things?"

"A partial list," she admitted. "But I've already indulged myself with a bath." She shifted slightly. "It's a good thing I didn't fall forward on my knees this afternoon. This way, I can hide my misery from the public," she told him dryly, alluding to the state of her posterior.

"I take it that's why you're not sitting."

Dara smiled grimly.

Ridge allowed his gaze to sweep over that portion of her anatomy. "Should we bring a pillow next time?"

Dara looked at him in horror. "And have the press plaster a shot of that on the comic page? I don't think so."

Strolling back into the room, he popped the top on a cola and handed it to her. "I'm supposed to guard your body, and believe me when I tell you, you've got a great—"

"I'll look after that part of my body myself, thank you very much," she quickly interjected. "I don't think it's your job to be quite so concerned with my..." She looked at the pizza, hoping it could provide her with a comfortable term, and waved the crust when she couldn't find one. "I believe my overall safety is your primary concern."

Wearing an enigmatic gaze, he crossed his arms and leaned against the sofa. "If you say so."

"So," she said firmly. Dara swallowed another bite of pizza and vowed to not let Ridge send her into another frenzy. If this scene was a little too cozy and if Ridge looked too appealing in his worn jeans and partially unbuttoned shirt, then it was just the dim light. In one quick movement, she flicked on the table lamp.

"Is your mother okay?" Ridge asked, watching her curiously as she turned on another light.

Dara nodded. "I'll call her more often during the next two weeks, though. She sounded a little lonely."

Ridge waited to see if she would add anything, but the only sound in the room was the muted volume of the TV. It took him a full moment before he realized that Dara was stealing covert glances of his chest. A rush of pure pleasure coursed through his blood. Heat swelled inside him, and fierce masculine pride nearly burst the rest of the buttons on his shirt. Just a couple of glances from beneath her eyelashes, he thought with disgust, and he was ready to rip off his shirt for her. He didn't even want to think about the state of the front of his jeans.

Inwardly cursing his hormones and ego, he cleared his throat. Twice.

Dara blinked. Ridge watched her cheeks bloom with vivid color. He wondered if the blush covered her whole body and thanked God that in America they didn't shoot a man for his thoughts.

"Sorry. Guess I'm more tired than I realized." She looked away and brushed her hair from her face. "I think I'll make an early night of it. Great pizza. It was nice of you to share." She moved toward her bedroom. "Good night."

"You don't have to—" Ridge stopped himself. Maybe it would be best if she went to bed *by herself*.

She whirled around quickly. "Oh, there is one other thing. Drew said we'll be taping an interview with MTV, so we'll be flying out to meet Harrison next—"

"Harrison," he repeated, the name a splash of cold water. Numbness spread through his limbs.

"Yes." Her dimple flashed disarmingly. "Harrison Montgomery, the next president of the United States of America. Our interview's next week. I guess you can swap horror stories with the Secret Service guys." She cocked her head to one side and her smile faded. "Let me know if you want to meet him. I'll introduce you."

Ridge shrugged, but didn't say a word. He couldn't have. Through the roaring in his brain, he watched Dara walk into her room and close the door. If he wanted to meet Harrison, she would introduce him. Her words echoed like a discordant refrain, and he wondered what Dara Seabrook would think if she knew she'd be introducing Ridge to his father.

Three

"It's gonna be a three-margarita night," Dara muttered under her breath as she stepped out of the limo door Ridge had opened for her. A group of Montgomery's supporters recognized her and gave a loud cheer. Ever mindful of the in-line skates dangling from her hand, Dara pushed her lips into a gracious smile and waved. "Four margaritas," she corrected herself.

"I don't want you going to a bar," Ridge said, walking with her toward the platform.

Dara cast her brilliant smile at him. "Tough," she returned cheerfully. Since that night he'd shared his pizza with her, he'd been about as warm and inviting as the planet Pluto. She wished she could dismiss him from her thoughts, but to her supreme irritation, Dara found she was aware of him every minute of the day. She was tired of walking on eggshells around Mr. All Business.

His gaze surveying the crowd, he frowned. "It's my job to keep you safe, and going to a bar—"

"Will give you a fresh challenge. I wouldn't want you to get bored."

He flicked an annoyed glance at her, then back to the crowd. "I pick the place."

Dara shrugged. "As long as they make great margaritas." And because she felt she'd been pushed just a little too far, she pushed back. "The jeans look great, Ridge," she said in a husky, taunting voice. "The women won't be able to keep their eyes off of you."

She saw him stiffen. When she'd noted his casual clothing and said she was relieved he wouldn't be carrying a weapon today, he corrected her and displayed the gun beneath his lightweight windbreaker. Although she found the weapon unsettling, she had to confess his jeans molded his masculine contours with breathtaking precision.

"Are you enjoying yourself?" he asked in the same soft yet lethal voice Dara remembered him using in the car when his hands had been on her thighs and his mouth had been too close—yet too far away.

A shiver ran through her, but she ignored it. After all, she was getting ready to make a complete fool of herself on all the major television networks. Dara gave him a reckless smile. "A woman has to take her pleasure where she can get it."

He'd sure as hell like to be the one to *give it* to her. Resisting the urge to pull his client into his arms and sling her over his shoulder, Ridge watched Dara sashay up the steps in front of him to the platform. With her feminine curves, the biker shorts and vibrant fitted top she wore were an unholy distraction he could ill afford.

Calling on years of discipline, he tore his gaze from her and back to the crowd. That was his job—to watch the crowd, not Dara. Her body might distract him, but it was her attitude that made him sweat. She was sexy, edgy, and a little careless. He could practically hear the ticking of a bomb ready to explode. She was pushing his hormones into overdrive and turning his hair prematurely gray. What was going on in her pretty, fiendish mind?

If he read her correctly, and he feared he did, Dara was spent. She'd had enough of the campaign. She'd had enough of the press. And she didn't like having a bodyguard. She'd been pushed one step over the line. Sweet Lord, Ridge wondered exactly how she was going to let it all rip.

It was almost enough to seduce his attention away from the upcoming MTV interview when he would see Harrison Montgomery face-to-face. But the prospect of seeing his father tightened Ridge's gut every time he thought of it. He'd expected his bitterness to increase, but not his curiosity about the bastard. His curiosity deepened with each passing moment, however, and Ridge hated that. Cramming his thoughts into the back of his mind, he nodded to Ray and ignored a blond woman's approving gaze.

The mayor greeted Dara, then introduced her over the loudspeaker. "We all know we're gathered here today to celebrate the renovation of our oldest park, Grayford Commons. The history of this park dates back to the revolutionary war. Your hard work and contributions have made Grayford Commons a place to be proud of again. We're especially honored today to have presidential candidate Harrison Montgomery's goddaughter—" The mayor grinned. "Dara Seabrook. She will lead our in-line skating parade and present the awards for the races. Please welcome Dara Seabrook."

Ridge slid a glance over to Dara and saw a trace of desperation she quickly disguised. "I didn't know I would be *leading* the parade," she said into the microphone, and waved her hand over the crowd. "Especially with all these fine in-line skaters ready to skate circles around me." She smiled. "I'm counting on you to skate circles around me, so someone will be handy to pick me up if I fall."

The crowd laughed. Dara commended the city on their renovation project and reminded everyone to vote for Montgomery, then made her way down the steps. Ridge took her arm.

"I can't believe they expect me to lead this," she whispered. "I'm going to kill Drew Forrester. Remind me of that when I see him, and don't let him talk me out of it."

Ridge bit the inside of his cheek in amusement, but kept his gaze on the crowd. Dara sank to the curb and began lacing her skates. "I've got a new guard named Ray on the other side of the street," Ridge reminded her. "Don't go too fast."

Feeling her tug at his pant leg, he spared her a quick glance. She shot him a dark glare. "That wasn't funny. You've seen me skate. I'm doing good if I remain vertical."

Helping her up, he placed a steadying hand at her waist. So, Darlin' Dara got cranky when she was nervous. "Maybe you'll surprise yourself."

"Not with these ankles," she said under her breath, then pushed off into the street. She still felt the warmth from Ridge's hand. He had a firm touch that, underneath it all, made her feel secure. Squashing the odd urge to turn around and ask him to take her away, she waved to the crowd and smiled brightly. She had a job to do, and comfort from Ridge Jackson wasn't on the agenda.

Within seconds a banner was thrust into her hand and she was surrounded by a group of elementary school children. To her right a band tuned up, but Dara didn't look. Keeping her gaze focused straight ahead and a smile plastered on her face demanded all her concentration.

She made it one whole block and unbent enough to exchange a few words with the children. By the end of the second block she was shakily humming to the band's accompaniment of "This Land is Your Land." Humming was safer because Dara always got the lines about the redwood forest, gulfstream waters, and the valleys all mixed up.

"Hey, lady," a little boy just behind her said. "Your knee pad's slippin'. You want me to get it for you?"

"Where?" Dara immediately looked down. The boy reached for her knee pad and ended up pushing her. Off-balance, Dara careened forward, the pavement coming closer at an alarming rate. "Oh!" Her right knee hit first, then her hands, and absolutely nothing diminished the impact. Pain vibrated through her leg and hands, then somebody fell on top of her.

"Watch out!" at least a dozen voices called as the skaters parted around her.

Mere seconds passed and Ridge was pulling her to her feet. She thought she heard him swearing, but the support from his body felt wonderful.

"Let's get you out of—"

"I'm sorry, lady." The little boy who had accidentally pushed her hung back from the rest of his friends.

"We need to move you," Ridge muttered, and began to guide her toward the curb.

"Wait a minute." Dara stopped as best as she could.

"I was just tryin' to help," the boy said, wringing his hands. "I didn't mean to push you."

Despite her throbbing knee, Dara's heart went out to him. No more than seven years old, he looked miserable. "Of course you didn't." She felt a trickle of blood run down her shin and bit her lip. "Tell you what. I need to get a bandage. Would you carry the banner for me?"

His brown eyes lit up. "Wow. Can I really?"

She ruffled his hair. "Really."

Ridge tugged her along. "Time to go," he said firmly. "I'll take you back to the limo and—"

Dara shook her head. "I can't leave yet. I've still got to present the awards for the in-line skating races." She gave a wry smile to the mayor who was bearing down on them, along with a half dozen other people. "Sorry about my little spill. Does anyone have a bandage?"

Within five minutes Dara traded her in-line skates for tennis shoes and had a bandage placed on her knee. While staying by her side for the next two hours, Ridge developed a healthy dose of respect for her. When he'd pointed out that no one would fault her for leaving early, she'd dismissed the option. "They're counting on me."

So he watched her smile and laugh even as she favored her right leg, and he thought that perhaps the statement about Dara being pure gold went deeper than the surface after all.

"Who's your sexy shadow?" Kit Brubaker, a longtime friend from Dara's alma mater asked as she gestured toward the waiter for a second round of margaritas.

"My bodyguard. Just until the end of the campaign." Dara licked the rest of the salt off the rim of her glass and sighed. It was such a relief to talk to someone not connected to the campaign. "My godfather insisted," she added, and glanced around. Ridge had selected well. The elegantly appointed hotel bar had great service and drinks. Of course, Ridge was far more pleased that the hotel had security and the hotel bar had security. Dara was beginning to feel as if Wells Fargo had taken over her life.

Kit's eyes widened. "A bodyguard. I can just hear Whitney Houston singing something sexy in the background!"

Dara didn't find that amusing. "Then you're suffering from delusions. Ridge is no Kevin Costner."

Kit glanced at Ridge again and nodded. "You're right. He's better looking than Kevin Costner."

Dara tried to affect a stern expression, but the combination of the eventful day and margarita were too much. She giggled past her frown. "You're right. He is better looking."

A gamine blonde who'd always been known for her sense of the absurd, Kit grinned. "So, what's it like having a bodyguard? Has he picked you up and carried you out of a crowd? Is he with you *every* minute of the day?"

Dara shook her head. "Did you get a part-time job with one of those scandal sheets?" she returned with a meaningful expression.

Kit's face softened in compassion. "You do have to think about the press all the time, don't you?" She gave a mild shudder. "I don't envy you that. But there's a reason they put you in front of a mike and camera, Dara. You're good."

"Thanks. You're nice to say that, although I'm not always sure exactly what I'm accomplishing." Dara gave a brief smile of gratitude to the waiter for the drinks. "It's not always bad, but we're at the end of the campaign right now, so the pressure to avoid any screwups is incredible." She took a sip. "That's why I called you. I knew I could count on my old sorority sister to help me blow off a little steam."

Kit placed a hand over her heart. "I'm honored, and I do take my duty seriously. But since it's not likely that I'll ever need a bodyguard, I hope you'll take pity on me and give me the dirt on what it's like to have one."

Dara sighed, but relented. Briefly glancing at Ridge, she thought about how she was always aware of him. The only respite she got was when she slept, and not always then. "He tells me what I can't do and where I can't go, which is just about anything and anywhere not preplanned. We disagree on how cautious I need to be. And you wouldn't believe the things he checks before I even enter a hotel building."

Kit looked disappointed. "This isn't nearly as exciting as I'd imagined," she confessed. "Have you had any personal conversations with him?"

"Not many. He's all business." Feeling a trace of guilt about discussing him, Dara lowered her voice even though she knew Ridge couldn't hear her. "He hovers—constantly."

Kit made a face and shrugged. "If he's that bad, why don't you ditch him?"

"My godfather won't fire him, so—"

"No." Kit shook her head emphatically. "I mean, if it's driving you nuts for him to hover, why don't you escape?"

Dara blinked at the suggestion. Alarm and a heady, naughty excitement shot through her. "You mean, sneak away without telling him? Sneak away to go shopping, or buy ice cream, or...?" Her list was endless.

"Or anything you want to do. You deserve it, Dara. You've worked like a dog during this campaign."

Why did she feel like she was talking to the devil himself? "Harrison would never approve."

"That's true," Kit admitted, but Dara also knew that Kit didn't give a damn about gaining the approval of others. In Dara's opinion, it was one of Kit's most admirable qualities.

"Clarence would probably have a stroke."

Kit nodded. "Yep."

"And it would infuriate Ridge." She took a sip of her drink and thought out loud, "The mature, responsible choice would be to continue to allow Ridge to do his job. Then, after the election, I'll be free to go where I please."

"Right. So what are you going to do?"

Wavering on her inclination to be mature and responsible, Dara smiled slowly. "That's a good question."

Ridge folded the last section of the newspaper, glanced at his watch, then at the door to Dara's bedroom. She'd mentioned something about sleeping in, but she'd never slept past eight-thirty before. He wondered if those margaritas were slowing her down this morning.

The phone rang, and since she had insisted, he waited for her to pick it up. He waited six rings and frowned. Why wasn't she answering? Was she sick? He'd put off checking on her because he didn't think the sight of Dara in bed would do a hell of a lot for his resolve to maintain a professional distance from her. Brushing that thought aside, he crossed the living room and was lifting his hand to tap on her bedroom door when he heard a knock on the suite door. Ridge turned away to answer it.

Newspapers clutched in both hands, Clarence Merriman burst in full of excitement. "How's our girl this morning? She must have been tired if she canceled our breakfast appointment. Have you seen these papers?" Clarence waved them in front of Ridge. "Drew Forrester is beside himself with joy. Said he tried to call Dara a few minutes ago and couldn't reach her. He told me to get her on the phone immediately, so he can congratulate her." Clarence winked knowingly. "I think he's got his eye on our Dara. Is she in the shower?"

Ridge's frown deepened. Drew Forrester was starting to get on his nerves, and he hadn't even met the man. "She's not in the shower." He shoved away from the doorway. "I was just getting ready to check on her."

Surprise crossed Clarence's face. "She's not up yet. That's not like Dara. I hope she's not sick."

Ridge tapped lightly on her door and waited a moment. Then he knocked a little more firmly. "Dara," he called. "Open up. Clarence is here."

He opened the door a crack, then pushed it the rest of the way open. Surveying her room in a one-second glance, he swore out loud. His chest squeezed tight.

Dara was gone.

His mind racing at the different possibilities, he dashed into the room and snatched up the note on her bed. As he read it, Ridge's alarm quickly shifted to anger. Clarence was talking a mile a minute. To halt the older man's panic attack, he shoved the note in his face, then immediately picked up the phone.

And while he dialed, Ridge thought about wringing Darlin' Dara's pretty little neck.

Anticipation shimmered throughout Dara. Five minutes to go. She adjusted her sunglasses and tugged the bill of her cap forward. The huge sunglasses were her own; the cap, one of the treasures she'd picked up at the flea market this morning. Her two hours of freedom had left her feeling more intoxicated than the margaritas from the night before.

It wasn't as if she'd done anything that bad—no illicit sex, no gambling, no criminal activities. She'd just spent the morning by herself shopping. Her final stop was the only ice-cream parlor in town that opened at 9:00 a.m. Dara wanted to eat two scoops of ice cream without being watched by Ridge.

The desire was becoming an obsession. Dara was dealing with a constant craving...which she had decided was Häagen-Dazs ice cream.

If the image of his nearly bare chest was branded on her brain, she conceded that it was just because, physically, Ridge was an incredible male specimen. And if her mind wandered too often to the question of just what it would be like to kiss his mouth and feel the passion rise within him, well, that was just one of the side effects of the stress from the campaign.

Dara smiled as the bell over the door announced the opening of the ice-cream parlor. The short, bald man wearing a wide, cheerful smile welcomed her. "Someone's been shopping at the flea market and decided she wanted ice cream for breakfast. What can I get for you?"

"You're so right. I'll take two scoops of Chocolate Chip Cookie Dough in a bowl. Thank you," she said as she took a seat in a white wrought-iron chair.

It couldn't have been more than a moment before the nice man served her ice cream at the table. Dara lifted a spoonful to her mouth and sighed. A spurt of triumph rushed through her. Mission accomplished.

Lifting the second spoonful to her mouth, she saw the ice-cream parlor door open. In walked a too familiar, tall, dark-haired man wearing jeans, a black leather jacket, and a midnight black scowl.

Dara's stomach sank with dread. Her spoon fell from her hand. She looked away. *Darn, darn, darn.* She hadn't planned on this. She needed a moment, just one moment . . .

He stopped directly in front of her table. Dara stared at his boots, and her throat tightened. Even they looked menacing. When she didn't acknowledge him, he dragged a chair right next to hers and sat entirely too close. She felt him lower his head and the combined scent of musky after-shave and angry male made her stomach knot.

"Well, Miss Seabrook," he said in a low, deceptively calm voice that sent an odd combination of heat and shivers through her, "have you been enjoying yourself?"

Four

———

"As a matter of fact, I have," Dara replied, shoving her spoon into her ice cream and finally lifting her chin to meet Ridge's gaze through her sunglasses. "How did you find me?"

Ridge lifted an eyebrow. Defiance oozed from her. He felt the kick of it right in his face. "Once I realized you were gone, it wasn't difficult. I traced the taxi through the hotel concierge, checked with a few flea-market vendors, and remembered you had a weakness for Häagen-Dazs ice cream." Still displeased that she'd slipped away, Ridge narrowed his eyes. "Clarence nearly had a heart attack."

Her defiant expression slipped a bit. "I'm sorry, but nobody needed to get upset. In my note, I told you when I'd be back. I'm twenty-five years old and perfectly capable of being on my own for a few hours."

"That's not the point. Until the end of the campaign, it's my job to make sure you're safe. You don't make it easy when you—"

"It isn't my job to make your job easy," she interrupted, lifting that chin again. "My job is to stay sane until the election, and I needed a break this morning. I feel crowded."

Seeing her shoulders stiffen with tension, Ridge thought she reminded him of a riled Thoroughbred. He deliberately gentled his voice. "Then you should have told me. I would have arranged a way for you to get away. Ray and I could watch you from a safe distance."

"I didn't want Ray watching me from a safe distance. I didn't want you watching me from a safe distance. I get tired of being watched all the time." She shook her head and pulled off her sunglasses. "But you wouldn't understand. You're able to cut off all your emotions or needs. It's always all business to you."

She seared him with the turbulence in her eyes. "I'm not like you. I need some time to myself. I need to do normal things—go shopping and eat ice cream."

Tilting her head to one side, she looked down her nose at him in what he would bet was a purely defensive gesture. She sure as hell hadn't ever done that to him before.

"Small pleasures, and I'm not sure you get the concept of pleasure," she said.

Her expression was finishing-school cool, but her tone was full of passion and a feminine confidence that made him want to teach her a thing or two. She lifted a spoonful of ice cream.

"Look away, Ridge. Your glare is melting my ice cream."

"Is this Dara's version of a temper tantrum?"

She sucked in a quick, short breath and glared at him. "I just needed to get away from ... my paid security."

A direct hit. Ridge took pride in handling his job with a minimum of customer dissatisfaction. Her attitude tore through his self-control. "This shouldn't be about you and me."

"It isn't. I was talking about pleasure," she said, her voice laced with the barest hint of feminine suggestion. "Something you don't understand."

Ridge felt his restraint pushed just a little further. He pried her fingers loose of the spoon and lifted it to her lips. "Open your mouth." He watched her eyes widen and felt a sense of satisfaction that he'd turned the tables on her. "You know, Dara, with all your talk of small pleasures, I wonder just how much you know about pleasure."

She opened her mouth to respond and he slipped in the ice cream.

"According to your file," he said, watching her cheeks flare with indignation, "you don't have a lot of experience with...pleasure."

She hated that file and he knew it. When she turned her head from his offering of more ice cream, he helped himself to the spoonful. Something about the action was oddly intimate. The same spoon had been in her mouth only seconds before.

Dara wanted to scream in frustration. Why was she so insatiably curious about this man? And what did she possibly hope to achieve by goading him? She didn't know the answers, but a forbidden anticipation was thrumming through her, as if a dam were getting ready to break. "I know what I like and what I don't."

"Maybe." He took another bite of ice cream. "Sometimes what we like and what we want isn't good for us. A man who loses himself in a woman's mind and body to the exclusion of everything else isn't good for anything."

Dara sighed impatiently. "I don't know what you're talking about, but you're eating *my* ice cream."

"I think you do know what I'm talking about." He extended the spoon to her again. When she hesitated, he moved his lips in a rare and dangerous I-dare-you grin. "Scared of my germs?"

Dara knew she was scared, but she wasn't sure if she was afraid of knowing Ridge intimately or never knowing more about him than she did now. Her fear had nothing to do with Ridge's germs. Holding his gaze, she played his game and accepted a mouthful of ice cream she didn't taste. She was too busy watching Ridge watch her. Too busy seeing his eyes darken when she curled her tongue under the spoon.

When she finished, he took a turn, and Dara felt an insidious heat burn inside her. "Why don't you just go ahead and kiss me and get it over with?"

The question had the effect of shattering glass. Ridge set the spoon down and stared at her for a long moment. He leaned closer. "Because I wouldn't want to stop with a kiss." His gaze trailed over her mouth and lower. "Because I've got a job to do, and it would be all too easy for me to get distracted by you."

It was a nice rejection, but it still stung. "All business," she said, and managed what she hoped was a cool smile. "I guess it's just as well. I need a man who can show me that he wants me."

His eyes flashed. "You need a man with a firm hand, for more than one reason."

"That's chauvinistic," she retorted, then pulled back. "But your opinion doesn't matter, because we don't really have a personal relationship."

"My life-style doesn't lend itself to entanglements," he said bluntly. "I need a woman tough enough to take it when it's all over and time to move on."

She paused, then backed down. "Well, that lets me out. I'm a soft touch." Her chest squeezed tight with a strange sense of disappointment, Dara stood, intending to leave. She looked for the manager, but he must have gone into the back room.

Ridge stood, his hand shooting out to clasp her wrist. "Why are you doing this?"

Looking at his large, strong hand, she hesitated. She had an overwhelming urge to slip into his arms. A knee-weakening thrill raced through her at the same time that her mind insisted she should just leave. How could she feel both bold and confused at the same time? It didn't make sense.

Why was she doing this? Why was she taunting him at every other turn? Stuck with honesty, she gently shook her wrist loose and slipped her fingers through his. "Maybe I just wonder what's beneath the super-bodyguard facade."

When he moved closer, her mouth went dry and her heart sped up. She took a breath, but it didn't seem to help, and for sanity's sake, she kept her gaze focused on a chip in the table. "Maybe I think about you too much," she whispered.

She felt his warm, strong palm beneath her chin. His touch was surprisingly gentle. When she finally met his gaze, she was struck by the wonder in his eyes.

He caressed her jaw and shook his head. "What are you doing to me, Darlin' Dara?" He ran his thumb over the seam of her lips, and she instinctively parted them, slipping her tongue out to taste his skin.

His eyes lit like twin golden flames, Ridge rubbed the pad of his thumb over her teeth. "What am I going to do with you?" he said low and deep.

Cupping her chin, he pulled her closer, inch by excruciating inch, until she could feel his breath but couldn't manage one of her own. Dara felt as if she'd been waiting for this, for him, for a very long time.

He brushed his mouth against hers, side to side, then dipped his tongue past her lips. She tasted a hint of sweet ice cream and a dark desire more heady than any margarita.

Closer... more. She was edgy with something that was just out of reach. The need to be closer, to feel more, pushed Dara close enough to feel the press of his hard chest against her breasts.

Ridge made a rough sound and deepened the kiss past testing, past playful, to outright sexual. The sliding thrust of his tongue was an explicit reminder of a more intimate act. The massaging motion of his fingers on her jaw made something inside her yield. An achy pressure built within her, from her lungs and belly to her breasts and lower still. Unable to stop, she lifted her hands, one to his rock-solid shoulder, the other to the back of his neck where her fingers slipped through his thick, soft hair.

Ridge groaned, and as if he'd been holding back, he slid his hand down to the small of her back, tilting her pelvis against his. A roaring need crashed through Dara, more powerful than she'd ever felt. The force of it buckled her knees.

Ridge caught her and gave a small shake of his head. With obvious reluctance, he slowly pulled his mouth away. "God, you're dangerous," he muttered, taking a deep breath.

Struggling for her own breath, Dara shook her head while his arms steadied her. "It's not me. It's—"

His gaze turbulent, he put his thumb over her moist lips to quiet her. "Remember what I told you. A man who allows himself to get lost in a woman to the exclusion of everything else isn't good for anything." Glancing around the ice-cream parlor, he swore softly and set her away from him. "The damn building could have fallen down for all I cared two minutes ago."

Dara couldn't agree with that last statement more, but when she saw the closed, hard expression on Ridge's face, her stomach took a deep plunge. "Is that so horrible? To want someone that much? To show it?" She swallowed over the lump in her throat. "In case you didn't notice, I was there, too. You weren't the only one participating."

"I noticed everything," he said, his eyes hot with unsatisfied passion, yet his face was as unyielding as steel. "But I'm here to protect you."

And not for anything else. Dara heard the unspoken words loud and clear, and felt the door shut in her face again.

Everyone was waiting for Montgomery.

Ridge told himself he wasn't genuinely curious, but the tension inside him told another story. Drawing a mind-clearing breath, he forced his confused emotions down into the black hole he'd created inside himself.

A couple of Secret Service agents who had given Ridge a nod of approval stood on either side of the MTV studio. Their gazes flicked over the young crowd, checking, Ridge was sure, for those telltale lumps and bumps in clothing that indicated a concealed weapon. The announcer had already given the audience their instructions, and there was a buzz of excitement rippling through the studio while the technicians and camera crew performed their preshow checks.

Ridge had spotted Clarence Merriman a few minutes ago. The man had been so nervous Ridge had wondered if he would fidget himself to death.

Glancing backstage again when he heard Dara's laughter, Ridge watched a woman dust a cosmetic brush across Dara's nose. Every time Ridge looked at her, he was reminded of what she'd felt like in his arms, how her lips had tasted, and how much he'd wanted a more intimate knowledge of her body. He was stuck with the memory and a gnawing desire that never seemed to quit.

Dara smiled her thanks to the makeup woman and turned her attention to a tall, meticulously groomed man in his mid-thirties who handed her a few sheets of paper.

Ridge knew the man from his pictures in the newspaper. Drew Forrester, Harrison Montgomery's crackerjack PR man, gave low-voiced instructions and Dara nodded, then hesitated. Looking up, she met Ridge's gaze and motioned him over.

"Ridge, this is Drew Forrester." She gave a cryptic smile. "I've mentioned him before."

"Yes. I recall his name." Ridge extended his hand. "Ridge Jackson." Ridge hadn't decided if he was glad to meet Drew yet, so he didn't add the perfunctory, "Nice to meet you."

Drew gave him an assessing look. "Your agency has an excellent reputation, and your file was very impressive."

"Wish I'd seen it," Dara muttered.

Drew patted her on the shoulder, but continued speaking to Ridge. "That bottle business gave us a fit with the press, so Harrison and I are relieved that someone of your caliber is in charge of Dara's security."

Ridge nodded at the same time he noted that Forrester didn't mention Dara's stitches, and Ridge decided then that he didn't like the man.

Drew smiled approvingly at Dara. "Speaking of the press, passing your flag to that little kid at the in-line skating parade was a stroke of genius. It made the six o'clock news on two of the networks and got some decent coverage in *People,* along with several newspapers."

Bemused, Dara shook her head. "Thanks, but I didn't really plan—"

"Good job." He squeezed her shoulder again and glanced back at his notebook.

Noting the quick flash of disillusionment in her eyes, Ridge felt a surge of protectiveness for Dara. "How's the knee?" he asked when Drew didn't. Her navy hose concealed her injury.

"Not sore anymore." She shared a commiserating smile with him and glanced down at her leg. "I've just got a colorful bruise and a scab a six-year-old would be proud of."

Tapping his pen against his notes, Drew frowned. "Now remember, these kids are a bit enamored with you. You might have to try to keep the focus on Harrison instead of—"

Dara's full, uninhibited laughter interrupted Drew midinstruction and tugged hard at something inside Ridge.

Frowning, Drew glanced around as if slightly self-conscious. "Why are you laughing?" he asked in a low voice.

She looked at him in disbelief. "Have you forgotten the Montgomery charisma? As soon as he enters the room, I'll be in the background—which is fine with me. Don't worry."

"This is a younger crowd."

"His appeal," she said in a mock dramatic tone, "crosses all economic and demographic lines. Wasn't that in one of your press releases? Stop worrying. You'll get an ulcer." Ridge saw the faintest trace of impatience flit across her face before she turned to him. "Drew says a few of us will be going out with Harrison for a late dinner after the taping, and—"

"Did I mention Harrison?" Drew smiled, all masculine charm now. "You deserve a night out, so I thought I would take you."

Glancing blankly at Ridge, Dara faltered. "I, uh..."

Ridge immediately sensed that she *didn't* want to go, which gave him an overwhelming but inexplicable sense of pleasure. "It's usually better if we have a little more lead time so I can check out the restaurant before Dara arrives," he said smoothly.

Drew's gaze met Ridge's. It hinted, just barely, of challenge. "Since she was coming with me, I didn't think she would need protection."

"Oh, no." Ridge smiled slightly, feeling a surge of some ancient drive involving territoriality. "I go wherever Dara goes. It's part of my job."

"Everywhere?"

"Everywhere." To diffuse the man's threatened ego, he added, "Just think of me as one of her accessories." Ridge shrugged as if he were harmless. "A purse."

Dara laughed, sharing his little joke. "A purse! Yes, an alligator purse." She glanced at Ridge and echoes of those moments in the ice-cream parlor filtered through her eyes and her face sobered. "An alligator with no leash."

Drew frowned. "If you don't like having this ... degree of security, perhaps I could try to arrange something else."

Silence followed, at least as much silence as there could be in the busy studio. Keeping his expression impassive, Ridge was surprised at the way his shoulders tensed. He felt Dara's gaze and met it, and the crazy connection between them seemed to stretch and pull at him.

Her eyes were filled with questions before she glanced down. "I've discussed it with Harrison. He thinks this is best."

Drew paused. "And what do you think?"

The question surprised both Ridge and Dara. He read the disconcerted expression on her face and reassessed Forrester. The man wasn't as insensitive as Ridge had originally thought. He was just focused on his job as Ridge was focused on his. Grimly, Ridge realized Forrester hadn't been distracted by Dara to the same extent that he had. Then again, he comforted himself, Forrester wasn't sleeping right outside her bedroom every night, either. Small comfort.

Drew reached for Dara's hand.

The sight irritated Ridge, but he didn't look away.

She shook her head. "We have three weeks until the election. I can't believe you're asking what I think of security when I'm having a tough time deciding what to wear on a daily basis."

The rare display of stress was evident in her tone. Ridge saw compassion cross Drew's face. "Sorry. You're so damn good at this that sometimes I forget what kind of toll it takes on you." He sighed. "It'll all be over soon. Maybe then—"

"Mr. Forrester." A woman with a cellular phone came toward him. "You've got a call."

Drew squeezed Dara's hand, then moved away. "It's always something," he muttered.

Dara watched him go, then tossed a quick surreptitious glance at Ridge before she gazed at her hands.

Ridge felt that humming thread between them again. "Busy man," he said, trying to get a fix on her.

She nodded.

"Thought you were gonna kill him."

She looked up. A slow, sensual smile tilted her lips, and the mischief came back in her eyes. As if she were sharing a secret, she leaned close and whispered, "There's still time."

Ridge wanted to kiss her.

He might have given in to the urge if he hadn't heard a loud voice announce, "Harrison Montgomery has arrived."

Dara stood, and within a minute Montgomery, shaking hands along the way, was walking toward them. The energy level in the room immediately jumped up two notches. With Secret Service suits on either side of him, Montgomery finally turned to Dara and swept her into a hug. Cameras flashed.

"How's my favorite goddaughter?"

As Ridge watched Dara return Harrison's embrace, the well of cynicism inside him, deepened by years of disillusionment, began to bubble like acid.

So this was his father.

He had one inch in height over Montgomery, Ridge estimated, and the knowledge absurdly pleased him. With silver hair and character lines, the senator's age was showing, but he wore it well. He exuded dignity, energy, and enough charisma, Ridge admitted grudgingly, to convert a roomful of atheists.

Ridge, however, knew he would not be one of the converts because he despised Harrison Montgomery.

Despite his hate, Ridge drank in his first face-to-face sight of Montgomery. He saw little resemblance between himself and Harrison except in build. Ridge had inherited his mother's dark hair, tan complexion, and full mouth.

So he'd gotten little of Montgomery, Ridge concluded wryly, certainly none of the man's charm.

"We're going to have to start giving you hazard pay," Montgomery said to Dara, shaking his head. "How's your knee?"

The affection and concern were in his voice. In other circumstances, Ridge might have thought the man was sincere.

Dara laughed and murmured something in response. It was obvious she felt a strong fondness for him. Her face lit up at his presence.

Ridge denied the quick spurt of envy that shot through him. Was he jealous because Dara freely showed her feelings for Montgomery, or because she had a closer relationship with his father than Ridge did? Neither, he assured himself, clamping his hard shell of reality back in place.

Nothing would develop between Ridge and Dara. Nothing could. And he despised Harrison Montgomery. After all, Harrison Montgomery had given him absolutely nothing but cause for bitterness. It was almost a relief to know he shared none of the man's physical, mental, or spiritual qualities.

At that moment the senator glanced up from Dara. Ridge met his gaze and the strangest sensation flipped his gut.

He might not share Montgomery's hair color or bone structure. He might not have the man's political savvy and charisma. He sure as hell didn't have the same kind of up-bringing.

But Ridge had his father's eyes.

Five

Somewhere above the roar in his ears, Ridge heard Dara. "Harrison, this is Ridge Jackson, my bodyguard."

"Good to meet you," Montgomery said, extending his hand. "Your record is excellent. It's a weight off my mind to know someone with your expertise is protecting my goddaughter."

Ridge merely nodded and shook his hand. What was he supposed to say? *Thanks, Dad.*

And then the moment was past. A moment he'd fantasized about as a child; the moment when his father said he'd been searching for his little boy and was so glad he'd finally found him. After his mother died, Ridge had fantasized about spitting in Montgomery's face and cursing him to the depths of hell.

Right now he was too numb to do either.

Ridge didn't draw a normal breath until Montgomery and *his goddaughter* had been urged toward the waiting crowd in the studio. A wave of sadness and anger flowed through his blood. He ruthlessly shook it off and took his position. Montgomery, be damned. Ridge still had a job to do.

They were a dream team in front of the audience, Ridge concluded dispassionately. Montgomery and Dara successfully fielded questions on everything from how to help the homeless to what kind of music they favored, what kind of underwear Montgomery preferred, and whether or not Dara had a special man in her life.

Dara had paused at that question and her gaze flickered uncertainly to Ridge.

The senator came to her rescue. "If she does, he'll have to get her godfather's approval."

The crowd laughed, and Ridge felt his gut squeeze tight at the fleeting vulnerability that darkened her eyes.

A young woman asked the next question. "Senator Montgomery, since you've never had any children, how can you truly understand and address the growing problems parents face with raising children in our modern society?"

Ridge went utterly still.

Montgomery's face reflected a hint of sadness. "It's true that Helen and I never had children, although we didn't lack for wanting them. Dara had been the daughter I never had, and I've been fortunate to be involved in every stage of her life since infancy." He smiled at Dara and patted her hand.

Ridge's stomach turned.

"I've never been homeless or disabled, but as president of the United States, it would be my duty to transcend gender, race, religion, and personal experience when I make policy. Fortunately, I've..."

Ridge didn't listen to the rest of the political rhetoric. As if a haze came over him, the studio seemed to fade away and he was in the shabby surroundings of his childhood

home with his mother while she shuddered through another drug-induced illness. It was to be her last. It was also
when she'd purged her venomous hate for Harrison
Montgomery by telling Ridge that he was Harrison's illegitimate son and that Harrison hadn't wanted him.

Ridge could blow a major pothole in Montgomery's
road to success if he came forward right now. The best
form of revenge against Montgomery would be exacted in
public. He didn't know exactly what held him back. The
idea tempted the darker side of him. When Ridge thought
of temptation, however, his mind naturally conjured up
Dara. He couldn't explain why his hunger for her had risen
to such a fierce intensity. It almost distracted him from his
driving need to make Harrison Montgomery pay.

Pushing it aside, Ridge focused on his last bleak memory of his mother. A cyclone of emotion instantly swirled
inside him. He recalled finding his mother the morning
after she'd told him who his father was. She'd been cold
and dead. He wished it had been Harrison.

The audience burst into applause, and Ridge's haze
cleared. Dara glanced at him and caught his gaze. She
smiled with relief as he felt the strange silken thread between them tugging at him again. Looking at her, he
wanted to feel her body pressed against his again, this time
in the dark with no one else around. This time he would
taste her skin and bury himself in her scent and softness.
This time he wouldn't stop until he knew her every way a
man wants to know a woman. There was something different about Dara. She was like a light, and when he was
with her, he felt like he'd spent his life in the dark.

Montgomery chose that moment to put his arm around
Dara. Ridge's gut clenched in response. He was torn between need and bitterness.

Dara couldn't stand another minute of the edginess inside her. Ridge had been silent and remote since they'd re-

turned from the studio. Clarence had left a few moments ago, and Ridge was still standing in the same position, facing the Manhattan skyline.

Away from her.

Although his behavior wasn't new, it bothered her more than usual. Her stomach knotted, and she berated herself for the response. Impatient, she resolved to take some sort of action. "I'm going to do a few laps in the pool," she announced, and took one last swallow from her glass of wine.

He turned around. "I thought you were tired."

She headed for her bedroom. "I am, but I think a few laps will help me sleep better tonight. If you don't want to go, call Ray," she said, half hoping Ridge would do just that.

"I'll go."

Her hand on the doorknob, she paused and looked back at him. This man was responsible for a great deal of her frustration and confusion; right now she didn't like him very much. "Fine. You're gonna burn up in that wool suit." And she hoped he did.

At the pool Ridge watched Dara moving from one end to the other with purposeful movements. She wasn't racing, but she wasn't playing, either. With her black maillot and wet hair hanging like a black silk curtain to her shoulders, she was slick and sexy.

He should have gotten Ray to spell him. Just this once. Instead, he watched.

She flipped over and started a well-paced backstroke. Every time she lifted her arm, her breasts arched upward, drawing his eyes to the feminine mounds. She flutter-kicked, and his gaze followed the natural progression to her hips and thighs. For a long moment he watched the juncture where her creamy thighs came together, and felt his loins harden with need.

Swearing, he forced himself to look away. She'd been right when she'd said he would burn up. He'd traded his suit for jeans and he was still hot. Hell, he admitted to himself, he'd be looking for ice even if he'd been buck naked. Hotter still if she'd decided to slip out of that body-caressing bit of a swimsuit. At least then he'd be able to do something about what she was doing to him.

Dara pulled one more lap, then switched to breast-stroke for two more. She wanted to be good and tired, so tired that when her head hit the pillow she would instantly fall into a dreamless sleep. Avoiding Ridge's gaze, she climbed the ladder and reached for her towel. "What did you think of the MTV special?" she asked to break the tight silence as she dried herself off.

Ridge shrugged. "It looked like it went well. The crowd loved you, and Montgomery probably picked up a few votes."

"Drew was ecstatic."

"I thought you were going to kill him," he reminded her again in a low voice as he led the way to the elevator.

Dara grinned despite her mood. "Since Harrison depends on him so much, I decided to spare him until after election day. I get the impression you don't like him much."

"I've never had much use for political types."

Dara nodded. She could see that. Ridge wasn't the type of man to appreciate guile and flattery. "Then what did you think of Harrison?"

He hesitated, and she watched his mouth stiffen. "He's a politician," he finally said, as if that explained everything.

They stepped into the elevator and Dara turned to him again. "I know it can be a sleazy profession, but someone's got to do it. Harrison's certainly got more character than most. He—"

"How do you know that?"

Dara met his hard gaze, wondering what on earth he was inferring. "I've known Harrison since I was a baby. He's always been there for me. There have even been times when my mother was sick and he took me into his home."

Ridge rested his hands on his hips. "But you haven't been with him every minute, have you?"

"Well, no, but—"

"Then you don't know what he's like when you're not around. You don't know what he's like with his business dealings. You don't know if he's ever made any under-the-table deals. For that matter, you don't know if his marriage is all it's cracked up to be."

Dara sucked in a shocked breath. "For Pete's sake, Harrison and Helen have been married for over thirty years!"

Something flashed in his eyes and was gone before she could identify it. "Some men are flexible on the interpretation of their wedding vows."

Dara just stared at him, numbly following him out of the elevator to her room. She prided herself on her complete belief in her godfather, but if there was one area that caused her an inkling of doubt, it was Harrison's relationship with his wife Helen. She couldn't exactly put her finger on why, but something about the careful way they interacted made her uncomfortable. She was being silly, she realized, and she would never confess her doubts to anyone else.

Angry that Ridge had so easily raised those doubts to the surface, she stepped through the doorway of the room and whipped around to face him. "You have a lot of nerve speculating on Harrison's character when you don't even know the man."

"As a voter, it's my privilege to speculate on the character of a man running for president," he replied in a cool voice as he closed the door. "Besides, you asked my opinion."

That comment merely made her more angry. "Well, maybe you're just assuming Harrison shares your own easy-come, easy-go opinion about women. At least he's maintained one solid relationship for most of his life."

"I wonder how many others he's had along the way," he said cynically.

"Maybe," Dara said, fighting fury, "it's none of your business." She took a deep breath and glared at him. "Maybe we'd better stop this discussion before I have to go back down to the pool and do some more laps. I needed to relax, and you're not helping one bit."

Stepping closer, he narrowed his eyes. "You started this discussion, and I didn't know it was part of my job to help you relax."

"Well, if it was, you sure as hell would have flunked. It would be easier to relax around the Gestapo!"

His jaw clenched and he took another step toward her, crowding her against the wall. His gaze traveled from her lips to her neck, then lingered on her breasts until she could practically feel his touch. To her mortification, her nipples strained against her damp swimsuit. She clutched her towel to her chest.

Ridge finally lifted his gaze. "If it's part of my job to help you relax," he said in a rough voice that had her heart tripping over itself, "say the word and I'll put every effort into accomplishing it." He put his hands on either side of her. "You know how I am about my work."

Dara's breath stuck in her throat. "What on earth are you talking about?"

"I mean, there's more than one way to relax." He grazed her chin with his finger.

His after-shave made her dizzy, but she understood what he was suggesting. Dara swallowed hard. "I thought you were determined to protect me—" She faltered, then went on. "Protect my body from yours."

His eyelids lowered. "I can protect you. I wouldn't hurt you," he said, emanating a powerful passion, a mixture of darkness and need.

Her mind was spinning, her body was thrumming. After struggling with her need every night for the past two weeks, she felt a ridiculous pang of uncertainty. "I thought you wanted to keep it all business between us," she whispered, wondering what had made him change his mind. "I thought you didn't feel anything for..."

"Say the word, Dara, and I'll show you what I'm feeling."

Her heart pounded so hard she wondered if it would crack a rib. He stroked her cheek, and she felt herself melting. "I feel..." She bit her lip and tried again. "I wish..." Knowing she wasn't making a bit of sense, Dara closed her eyes. "I don't know," she whispered weakly.

"Then I'll tell you what I want." He nuzzled her damp ear. "I want to kiss you." He pressed his lips to her temple where her pulse flickered double time.

Dara opened her eyes and looked into his. They were hot, predatory, aroused, and arousing. "Yes," she said huskily.

He leaned closer and reached for the towel. "I don't want anything between us. Do you?"

Slowly shaking her head, she released the towel. His gaze still holding hers, he dropped it behind him and lowered his head.

His lips slid over hers with silken certainty, and Dara's body was immediately thrown into a state of heated anticipation. He nibbled and caressed, seducing her response. Sucking gently on her mouth, he sneaked his tongue past her lips and Dara mirrored his every movement in return. She wanted to taste him. She wanted to feel him. She wanted to know him.

He took another step closer and Dara had the sensation of being surrounded. The wall was cool at her back and

Ridge, all heat and strength, covered the front of her. She didn't feel threatened, she felt protected.

Angling her chin with his hand, he deepened the kiss and pressed his chest to her sensitive breasts. Her nipples tingled with every subtle movement he made. His fingers caressed their way down her neck and shoulders until he hooked his thumbs under her arms and, skimming the underside, nudged them up around his neck. The position shifted her balance so that her pelvis tilted into his hardened masculinity.

"Oh," she exclaimed against his open mouth, tightening her hands on his shoulders.

"Good," he growled, and rocked gently against her.

Every feminine nerve ending clenched in response. A wave of heat singed her skin and sent her blood roaring through her bloodstream. Her arousal was so swift and intense she struggled for her equilibrium.

His finger's lazy slide back and forth on her shoulder beneath the strap of her swimsuit distracted her from her uncertainty. When he skimmed that lazy, impertinent finger down her chest to her breast, almost to her nipple, a small helpless sound found its way out of her throat.

Ridge immediately eased back. "Too fast?" he murmured, and put his arms around her. It took a moment before she realized he was hugging her. Heat and need emanated from him, but now there was tenderness. She sighed. That quickly, he reassured her.

Her heart swelling in her chest, she stretched against him and pressed her mouth to his throat.

Swearing softly, he tensed. "Dara, you're sending mixed signals."

Feeling the touch of her tongue against his skin, Ridge swore again. He was burning up from the inside out. "Dara." He injected a note of warning in his tone. "Talk to me."

She made a soft sound of frustration and ducked her head. "Do I have to explain?"

Her fingers toyed with his hair. "This is so embarrassing," she whispered, and gave a little groan. "I've never been this—"

Wondering what in heaven or hell was going on inside her, Ridge nudged her chin up and stared. What he saw made his pulse throb in every erogenous zone of his body. Her hooded eyes were nearly black with arousal, her cheeks were flushed, and her lips were sensuously swollen from his kiss. He swallowed past the sudden dryness in his mouth. "You've never been this what?"

She bit her lip, and he stifled a groan.

"This hot." Uncertainty crossing her features, she glanced down. "It's a little . . . scary."

The last word was so low and muffled he barely heard it, but she might as well have given him a double punch in the gut. Her obvious arousal fed his own.

Her honest dismay at the strength of her response to him, however, knocked him on his butt, and Ridge, who had never adored anyone, thought Dara must be the most adorable woman ever created. Curled against him, she was all vulnerable, soft femininity when he was rampant need. By the little shudder running through her, he saw that he wasn't the only one, though, having problems with the need.

He threaded one of his hands through her hair and gently urged her gaze back to his. "Scary or exciting?"

"So exciting it's scary," she managed, her eyes telling him she wanted him so much it hurt.

A crazy kind of exultation set his heart racing. Ridge felt the beginnings of a grin. "Then maybe we should just stick to kissing for now." He met her uptilted mouth. With his lips touching hers, she immediately opened to him and Ridge fed off of her sweetness.

She knocked his equilibrium into another galaxy when she sucked gently on his mouth and twisted against him. His gentle amusement faded, along with his confidence that he could keep everything under control. His arousal strained against the notch of her thighs and she spread her legs to accommodate him. When she wrapped her tongue around his, she might as well have been stroking his thickened masculinity.

The turmoil of meeting Montgomery face-to-face drove him on. Darkness rode on his shoulder. Ridge wanted more. He needed to push back the pain, and Dara was pure pleasure. "Let me touch you." His mouth still joined with hers, he pushed the straps down on her bathing suit. She made a mild protest when he momentarily pulled her arms away from him to slip the straps the rest of the way down, but when he cupped her breast in his palm, she moaned in pleasure.

That little moan was like gasoline to the fire.

His libido shot through the roof.

Her hands went wild.

She tugged the buttons loose on his shirt and pushed it apart and Ridge pulled her against him. Her bare breasts rubbed against his chest, sending a shower of sparks through his bloodstream. For all of three seconds he was in heaven.

But then he wanted more.

He lowered his head and took her breast into his mouth. Dara gasped.

Desire gnawing at him, he made himself pull away. "Too much?" he asked in a rough voice as he indulged in the sight of her bare torso. Her breasts were full, her nipples like raspberries on cream.

Dara moved her head in a circle, her wide eyes imploring him. "Don't stop," she choked.

The undiluted need to claim nearly sent him pushing her down to the floor. He struggled with himself. *Damn, he wanted her.* Cupping her breast, he suckled the tight tip and swirled his tongue around it. She trembled and a bead of perspiration trailed down his back. "I want to touch you more," he muttered, skimming his hand to the top of her thighs.

Holding her breath, Dara felt his finger slip beneath the edge of her swimsuit to where she was moist and wanting. She bit her lip and waited.

Ridge took her mouth again at the same time his fingers explored her intimately. Perhaps at another time her mind might have rebelled against it, but for this moment her heart knew him. He was her protector, her keeper, her lover. His thumb found her most sensitive cleft while his finger slipped inside her, and Dara turned to pure liquid. She was no longer substance, not flesh and bone. She was just sensation. She had never felt like this.

The room slipped away and her only reality became Ridge, his broken breaths, his musky, male scent, his mouth, and his hands. Heaven help her, he was taking her somewhere she'd never been before. But she needed to touch him. She needed a deeper intimacy with him.

Reaching for the snap of his jeans, she fumbled as she edged the zipper down and wrapped her hands around his fullness.

Ridge groaned, momentarily pausing in his ardent caresses. He felt like steel encased in velvet. When she stroked him, he swore, but didn't remove her hand. "We've gone way past kissing," he muttered as if he felt he needed to warn her.

His thumb grazed that tiny pearl of sensation and Dara shuddered. Sexual instinct, as old and strong as time, made her caress him again.

He let out a hissing breath and stopped her. His eyes were pure topaz fire. "I can't promise you what will happen if you don't stop."

Dara didn't care. It was as if her body and heart had taken over. She was reaching for something…for her, for him, and it had gone too far to stop. Holding his gaze, Dara slipped her finger over his honeyed tip.

His nostrils flared as he sucked in a short, quick breath. Ridge swore and rocked his lower body searchingly against hers. "What are you doing to me?" he asked against her mouth.

"The same thing you're doing to me."

Dara could practically hear Ridge's restraint tear in two. His hands and mouth claimed her with ruthless intimate persistence, and the room spun. He stroked, and because she needed to touch him, she caressed him, too. She was certain her technique didn't match his, but he didn't seem to mind. She moved in a matching rhythm with him.

The tightening coil inside her expanded, and her body clenched in a mind-melting spasm that shook her to the bone. She cried out his name at the same time he jerked convulsively against her and spilled himself into her hand.

Dara's knees promptly buckled beneath her.

Ridge caught her up against his chest and she felt the pounding vibration of his heart against her cheek. Her center of gravity was shot. She wasn't sure which way was up and which way was down. "Oh, Ridge," she murmured helplessly as she fought for breath.

"Yeah" was all he could manage. His voice a growl, he tightened his embrace as he struggled for his own breath. The muscles in his thighs were rippling as if he'd just run a marathon. Dara Seabrook had just given him the most erotic experience of his life. His head couldn't hold it all. His strongest urge was to carry her into her bedroom and lock the door behind them. Another fainter instinct that reeked of survival suggested that he'd just made the biggest mistake of his life. With Dara wrapped around him like a satin sheet, however, he kept thinking about everything he hadn't done with her that he still wanted to do. And all that he wanted to do again.

"How come your legs work and mine don't?"

She sounded so genuinely perplexed he chuckled. "Don't ask me to walk."

"But you're standing unaided."

"Yeah, but that's about all."

She glanced up then, and he touched the curve of her cheek. "Why are my ears ringing?"

Listening, he paused for a moment. "That's the phone."

"Oh." Her voice was full of relief.

"We should get it," Ridge commented, but made no move in that direction. The motion of moving away from her was intolerable.

"How?" she asked weakly.

His heart lightened, and he chuckled again. "Like this." Scooping her into his arms, he carried her through her bedroom to the plush bathroom and set her on the large vanity next to the sink. The phone continued to ring as he dampened a washcloth and handed it to her. "I'll pick it up in the bedroom." He paused a half second. "And I'll tell whoever it is to call back tomorrow."

Dara met his gaze and felt a dip in her stomach at the promise she saw in his leonine eyes and the suggestion she heard in his voice. His gaze hovered over her still bare breasts with masculine approval.

There would be more.

Pressing the cool cloth to her forehead, she swallowed over the lump of anticipation in her throat and just nodded. While he walked away, Dara tried to get her bearings. She felt as if an explosion had gone off inside her, around her. As far as she was concerned, the hotel room should be a pile of rubble.

She was stunned by the intensity of their physical passion. There'd been no desire for half measures, no tender, polite testing, from her or him. When he'd kissed her, it had been like going from zero to blast-off. Her heart was still racing.

Get a grip. Dara stuck her trembling hands under the faucet. His scent was all around her. An odd part of her didn't want to wash it away. Her brain was slowly starting to kick in and she heard the insistent voice of reason telling her she had lost her mind. After all, hadn't she learned that Ridge was a man unto himself, a man who made emotional connections with no one? Hadn't he told her that in no uncertain terms? What was she doing giving her body and heart to such a man?

She heard the deep rumble of Ridge's voice and it reminded her of the low, sexy sound he'd made when he'd held her and she'd held him. Her body shuddered in response. She was a mass of want and doubt, need and uncertainty. Torn in opposite directions, Dara pulled up her bathing suit and splashed her face with water.

A heartbeat later Ridge appeared in the doorway. She didn't know what to do, she just knew she still wanted him with a power that frightened her. But Ridge's eyes were flat, and his mouth hard. Despite her confusion, Dara felt her stomach take a plunge. He'd put the distance between them again. The wall was up. Her mind scrambled to determine why.

"Your godfather wants to talk to you," he told her in an expressionless voice, and extended the cordless phone to her.

Dara just stared blankly at him.

He waited a moment, then impatiently pressed the receiver into her hand. "Here," he said.

Then he walked out of the room. Dara bit her lip at an inexplicable sense of loss. She knew he wouldn't be coming back. Not tonight. Not ever.

Six

___

"Here's the latest," Clarence said triumphantly, lifting the newspaper article for Dara's view. "One of President Pierson's campaign aides has abandoned ship."

Dara felt only the mildest interest. She was too aware of Ridge's heavy silence. He'd barely spoken to her this morning. "'Beth Langdon,'" she read the woman's name out loud, turning her attention to the article. "It says she recently got married in France." Feeling an errant trace of envy, Dara tried to place the woman. "Wasn't she the one who was pushing for the homeless bill?"

Clarence nodded. "Now she's making noises that Pierson has no intention of doing everything he promises." The older man snorted. "As if that's news to the rest of us."

"There was something about her I liked. She wasn't quite so slick. She seemed intelligent and caring."

"Well, of course she's intelligent if she's figured out Pierson."

Dara gave Clarence a sideways glance. "I agreed with her on the homeless issue."

Clarence looked appalled. "Do you realize how much that bill would cost the American taxpayers?"

"Do you realize what a waste it is to leave these people on the street?"

Clarence shook his head. "You've misunderstood. I'll provide you with Harrison's research and—"

"I know what Harrison's platform is," she said wearily, and stood. "In this instance, I just don't necessarily agree." She felt a tinge of impatience at Clarence's alarmed expression. "Oh, don't worry. I'll keep it to myself. I understand my job. I'm supposed to represent Harrison. If I have any bones to pick with him, I'll do it in private if at all."

"Well," Clarence said, his bluster deflating like a withering balloon. "I'm glad to hear that." He cleared his throat and checked his watch. "Since we're leaving in about an hour, I'll make a few phone calls."

Dara didn't want to take out her frustration on Clarence. She gave the older man a quick hug. "Don't mind me. I woke up on the wrong side of the bed."

His round face crinkled in concern as he walked out the door. "Maybe you can get some rest on the plane. Your itinerary for the next few days is going to be very tight."

She nodded. "That's right. Besides the two outdoor rallies, I've got the Hope for Sunshine charity event. I'll try to relax on the plane."

But Dara wasn't sure rest was what she needed.

Feeling Ridge's presence behind her, she wondered where her surge of rebelliousness had come from. Was it end-of-the-campaign nerves, of the result of Harrison's telephone call last night? He'd been checking on her. He wanted to know if she was still unhappy with her bodyguard. She'd managed to tell him that she and Ridge had come to a meeting of the minds. She had not told him that they'd also nearly come to a joining of their bodies.

Harrison had asked a few more questions about Ridge, questions she couldn't answer. The fact that she knew so little about Ridge was like coarse sandpaper rubbing over her skin. Dara had lost patience, something she never did with Harrison, and asked, "Why don't you check his file?"

She remembered her godfather's long silence, her quick spurt of guilt, and subsequent unwillingness to give in to anything that even hinted of manipulation at that moment. She already felt out of control.

She sighed and turned around, catching him staring at her from hooded eyes while he sat on the sofa. He quickly looked away. Pride would have her competing with Ridge for who could out-ignore the other, but Dara just didn't have the energy for it. "Are we going to pretend nothing happened last night?"

Ridge looked up from the sheet of paper he'd been writing on. "Nothing should have."

She walked toward him and sat on the opposite side of the coffee table. The lovely Queen Anne chair offered little comfort. She folded her hands together. "But something *did.*"

Ridge narrowed his eyes, but Dara thought she saw a flash of guilt. "The proximity finally got to us. Things got out of control. It was a mistake."

How simple. He was so calm, and she wanted to scream. Dara took a deep breath. "You sound as if you've had experience with this kind of situation before." She tried, but couldn't quite keep the edge from her voice. "Have you had similar problems with your other clients?"

"No," he admitted reluctantly, "but I think we've established that you're not exactly a typical client." He tossed down his pen in frustration. "For God's sake, Dara, you were wearing a bathing suit that would bring the entire American male population to their knees."

"So, it was just the bathing suit?"

Ridge threaded his hand through his hair. "Why are you doing this?"

"Because I couldn't walk for ten minutes after you finished with me. Because I smelled your scent and felt the imprint of your mouth and hands on me. Because..." she said, her voice cracking, "I let you get close to me."

The accusation in her blue eyes made his gut knot. Ridge had stayed awake the whole night and tortured himself with the image of her every soft sigh and gasp. His jaw worked in frustration. When he'd formulated his plan of revenge against Montgomery, he hadn't counted on his world being rocked by Dara. He couldn't let his unexpected feelings for her change his course of action. Nothing could ever come of a relationship between them. He knew it. He'd always known it. When Montgomery had called last night, the futility of it might as well have been written in stone. His bleak gaze tangled with hers, and he shook his head. "I'm sor—"

"Don't you dare apologize," she cut in, her voice both oddly husky and ruthless. He saw the sheen of tears and her struggle to contain them. His hands tightened with the need to hold her.

She took a deep, audible breath. "It's insulting enough for you to call it a mistake. If you said you were sorry that you kissed me and held me, sorry that you let me touch you, I might just have to slap you." Her voice trembled. "And you'd have to stop me."

She stood with regal dignity and walked away. Ridge felt like the lowest scum ever created. He wished she would slap him. He sure as hell wouldn't stop her.

They traveled to Virginia for the last stretch of the campaign, and though she seemed to pull back, Dara didn't ignore Ridge or cut him to shreds by word or deed. She was merely impeccably polite. Ridge struggled with a sense of loss, but told himself this way was best.

At Dara's sprawling, Georgian-style childhood home in Middleburg, the Seabrooks' longtime housekeeper, Rainy, greeted Dara with a hug and welcomed Ridge, Clarence, and Ray. After guiding the men to their rooms and going over the schedule for meals, Rainy and Dara spent an hour catching up.

They'd barely settled in before Dara was skipping dinner to go out again. Decked out in a little black dress with a white satin collar, she strode past Ridge, leaving her favorite scent in her wake.

Ridge caught her as she reached for her coat at the front closet. "Where are you going? There's nothing scheduled for tonight."

She didn't pause. "It's a charity benefit. It has nothing to do with the campaign, so you don't really have to go."

Ridge frowned and helped her into her coat. "Why wasn't it on my agenda?"

She gave her hair a quick toss from beneath the coat collar. "I guess because this one isn't for the campaign. This one is for me."

"A date?"

"No." She sighed and gave up avoiding his gaze. "Look, it's no big deal. The local ladies club is holding a little talent and fashion show to benefit children of adults with chronic mental illness. I met one of the organizers last year at my mother's residential treatment center and she asked me to emcee. The chauffeur will take me and wait there, so you can take a break. You don't need to baby-sit tonight."

He could argue the comparison about *baby*-sitting until doomsday. The deep neck of the dress showed enough cleavage to remind him how her full, soft breasts had felt in his hands and against his chest. Her lips were strawberry red, but it was her eyes that pulled at his midsection. Dark blue and full of all the secrets she was trying to hide from him—because he'd hurt her. The knot in his gut tightened. "I take a break when you take a break. What time do you have to be there?"

"You're impossible." Dara lifted her hand in exasperation. "I would argue with you about this, but I assume I would be wasting my energy."

Ridge fought the grin that tugged at the edge of his mouth. "You assume correctly. What time?"

"I need to leave in about two minutes." She gave him a swift once-over that made his temperature rise. "The jeans will have to go."

Five suggestive responses raced through his mind. His libido would just love to shuck his jeans along with her dress and whatever else she was wearing beneath it and pick up where they'd left off the other night. Cursing his vivid memory, Ridge bit his tongue and turned away. "Two minutes," he muttered.

Within a half hour they arrived at the hotel hosting the event. After Dara got out of the car, she took Ridge's arm. "We need to settle something."

Hearing the tension in her voice, he nodded and led her through the hotel entrance. Although he stood beside her, his gaze was on the crowd. "Go ahead."

"I don't want a bodyguard for tonight. I—"

Impatient, Ridge interrupted. "We've discussed this before."

"This time is different. What I'm doing tonight has nothing to do with the campaign."

He narrowed his eyes. "It's still on my clock. I keep you safe until after election day."

Dara swore softly. "Would you just look at me and listen?"

The rare sound of her cursing clued him in that the nerves she exhibited were just the tip of the iceberg. Cautiously, Ridge turned to her.

Her eyebrows knitted in frustration. "There will be children here tonight. I don't want you pulling out your gun and scaring them."

That pinched his ego. "I don't make a habit of scaring children."

"I'm sure you don't intend to." Dara bit her lip and briefly glanced away. "I'm not handling this well," she murmured more to herself than to him. "I know several of these people socially, so I'm not comfortable with doing things the way we usually do them."

"What do you mean?"

She flipped her hair behind her ear in a gesture that he'd seen her do when she was flustered. "I mean, I don't want to have to explain the presence of a bodyguard to everyone. It would distract from what I'm trying to do here."

Ridge hardened his voice. "I'm not leaving."

"I didn't ask you to leave! I just—" She swore again and held her breath as if she were struggling for patience. "I realize this may be difficult, but I prefer to introduce you as my escort rather than as my bodyguard. That means you'll need to exhibit a few social graces." Her voice cooled considerably, and she wore that finishing-school, pissed-off expression on her face. "Your toughest challenge is that you will have to pretend to like me." She gave him another once-over; this one made his hand itch to paddle her fanny. "Think you're up to it?"

The trace of insolence in her eyes and tone might have offended Ridge, but God help him, he found it sexy. He took her hand, folded it inside his arm, and lowered his head. "Dara, I've never gotten any complaints about not being up to it."

Dara gulped. Her rash innuendo had blown up in her face. She should have kept a rein on her temper. His sug-

gestive retort shouldn't have surprised her. Being this close
to Ridge wasn't difficult.

It was impossible.

His proximity turned her nervous system upside down.
His predatory gaze made her feel like she'd just stepped off
a cliff. Her cheeks blistered with heat, and her poor, piti-
ful brain moved with the speed of an eensy-weensy spider
climbing up a waterspout. Taking a shaky, shallow breath
because she surely couldn't have managed a deep one, she
stretched her lips into what she hoped resembled a smile.

Sanity, she urged. *He's played yo-yo with you before.*
She wished she wasn't trembling. Pulling back, she un-
glued her tongue from the roof of her mouth. "No complaints?" she managed, relieved that her voice was near
normal. "Let's hope your record holds."

For the rest of the evening, Ridge exhibited a side she'd
never seen before. Cordial to the ladies, polite to the men,
and surprisingly charming with children. Backstage, as she
glanced through her script, she watched him a few feet
away.

A five-year-old boy tugged uncomfortably with his bow
tie. "These clothes are dumb."

Bending down, Ridge grinned and straightened the tie.
"It'll all be over before you know it. Then," he said in a
conspiratorial tone, "I hear you get to eat as many cookies as you want."

The little boy's eyes widened like saucers. "As many as
I want. I'm gonna eat ten." He spun around to share the
good news with his friends.

Dara shook her head chidingly. "His parents are not
going to be happy."

Ridge stood and shrugged. "He'll stop at five. Anticipation's half the fun." He glanced at his watch. "The show
starts in about five minutes. What can I get you to drink?"

Dara gathered her papers. "I've got water. You don't
have to—"

He put his hand over the papers. "You know, you really shouldn't discourage us crude bastard types when we're trying to exhibit a few social graces."

"I never called you a crude bastard," she said.

His gaze locked with hers for a long moment, and she feared he could see things she wanted to hide. "And you never would," he acknowledged quietly. "Even if it was the truth." His gaze dropped to her mouth. "Maybe that's why it's not hard to pretend to like you, Dara. So what do you want to drink?"

Dara swallowed. She felt herself soften toward him. It was involuntary and instinctive. Compelled to soothe the pain behind his cynicism, she reached her hand out to his. "It's not the truth."

He laced his fingers through hers. "Before I met you, I had you pegged—all show, no substance. That wasn't the truth, either."

Dara felt a surge of tenderness. How she longed for the touch of his hand and lips. He had become her constant craving. One she was forced to deny. She wanted to lean closer, to press her mouth to his jaw, to drown in the sensation of being held by him. Her protective mechanisms yelled foul. Her pulse was skittering at superspeed.

Dara pulled her hand away, but the sensation of the calluses on his palm lingered. "I'll take iced tea, heavy on the ice." She made herself look away from him as he went to the bar.

The program went off without too many blips. One little girl lost her sense of humor halfway down the runway and started bawling. After making a joke about how tights and panty hose can make the best of us cranky, Dara picked up the toddler and offered her some juice. Two elementary school age boys livened things up with a karate demonstration complete with kicks and yells.

The program ended with an original poem read by a young teenage girl. In a soft yet clear voice, she told the story of shattered dreams and fear. Ridge was surprised by how her tale called up memories of his own childhood. The loneliness and confusion could have been yesterday. He saw Dara listening with her heart in her eyes. Her body was tense, her hands knotted together at her waist.

Now he understood another part of the reason she'd been so flustered earlier. There was no way she could do this benefit without feeling like she was walking through an emotional mine field. Hell, he was struggling with his own baggage. A fist of protectiveness squeezed his heart. This was one time Dara should have said no.

He watched her discreetly brush tears from her eyes before she embraced the teenager. Then she led the audience in a round of applause that grew to a standing ovation. He wondered if anyone else saw the weariness etched across her face. He wondered why he did.

After the clapping ceased, the press surged forward. Moving away from his position behind the stage, Ridge immediately stepped closer to Dara.

"Miss Seabrook, what do you think about the recent fluctuation in the polls?"

Dara hesitated before she shifted into her public persona. Ridge could practically hear the grinding of the gears. "Polls are supposed to fluctuate," she said. "I'm pleased that Harrison Montgomery is still well in the lead."

"Will Senator Montgomery alter his strategy as we get closer to election day?"

"Not to my knowledge. But. . ." she said, shaking her head when another reporter raised his hand to ask a question. "I'm not here to discuss the election tonight. I'm here on behalf of this great group of kids. The coordinator, Sylvia Turner, will be happy to answer your questions and," she added meaningfully with a broad smile, "accept your generous contributions." Her blatant bid for donations sent a ripple of good-natured laughter through the crowd. She handed the microphone to the coordinator and turned to Ridge.

"Ready to go?" he asked in a low voice.

When he offered his hand, Dara took it without hesitation. "Yes." She couldn't remember when she'd felt this tired. It was beyond physical. She felt as if she had handed over all her defenses and now that she needed them back, she couldn't find a single one of them.

Ridge snatched her coat from a hanger backstage and wrapped it around her.

"Thanks," she murmured, feeling his gaze intent and searching on her. She managed a few parting words with some of the children, but the exhaustion was pulling hard.

"The limo's out back," Ridge said, and put his arm around her.

Drawing in a deep breath, Dara struggled with the urge to bury her face in his neck, to wrap herself in his strength. His comfort stemmed from his role as escort, Dara reminded herself. As they stepped into the night air she realized she should remind herself that Ridge didn't really care about her, but for this moment she was thankful for the farce.

He tucked her into the limo, and Dara immediately felt herself melt into the upholstery. She had the odd sensation of feeling her surroundings spin though she knew she was sitting perfectly still.

"Are you gonna be okay?" One hand on the top of the car, he leaned closer and looked at her again. "Alone?" he clarified when she didn't answer.

Taken off guard by his sensitivity and the warmth in his eyes, Dara blinked. She had trouble coming up with a quick response. "I, uh..."

Signaling the chauffeur, Ridge swung into the seat beside her instead of riding in front and made the decision for her. "Let me fix you a drink," he muttered.

He slammed the car door closed and Dara leaned her head back against the seat. Still chilled, she pulled her coat around her. "You already did that tonight. Besides, there are no margaritas in the bar."

He bent over, searching through the various bottles of liquor. "Whiskey, bourbon, gin." He glanced at her. "You don't drink much of the hard stuff, do you?"

Still trying to put a mental bandage on wounds reopened during the benefit, she rolled her head from side to side.

"Here's some red wine that hasn't been opened." He opened the bottle and poured some of the red liquid into a plastic tumbler.

"I don't really—"

"Yeah, well drink it anyway. Your face looks like chalk."

Dara reluctantly accepted the wine. "You sound like Clarence." She took a few sips and watched him adjust the thermostat.

Ignoring her comment, Ridge turned back around and studied her. "Why did you agree to do this benefit?"

Hearing the disapproval in his voice, she felt another start of surprise. "You know about my mother. It was natural for me to get involved."

He shook his head. "Didn't you think about all the memories this kind of thing would dredge up? With the campaign, you've been going nonstop. From where I sit, you're running close to empty."

He was right on the money. Dara took another sip and closed her eyes. "I was hoping it didn't show."

"It probably doesn't to most people, but I see you day-in and day-out. I'd have to be blind not to notice that you're rough around the edges." He sighed. "You can't say yes to everyone. They'll run you until you're not good for anything."

Distress tightened her chest. It was true. The nonstop pressure of living a mistake-free life was wearing on her. But Dara knew there was a lot riding on her performance. Harrison was counting on her, and she didn't want to let him down. She didn't want to let anyone down. Was it that obvious? Dara wondered. She looked at Ridge. She knew she was having a tough time holding it together, but she'd thought she covered it well. "Are you saying I'm not good for anything *now?*" She abhorred the quiver in her voice.

Ridge swore. "No. I just think you should have let someone else handle the benefit tonight."

"I really couldn't. I promised them last year and—" She pressed her lips together and searched his eyes for understanding. "I was okay until the poem." A knot swelled in the back of her throat. "I tried not to think about my mother, but all these emotions came up and before I knew it, I was crying." She felt wetness threaten and pressed her fingers to the corners of her eyes and turned her head. "Like I am now. I'm sorry." God, she felt embarrassed, but the tears kept coming. "I should have warned you I'd be horrible company," she choked.

His hands on her shoulders, he urged her back around. "You'd have to work at it pretty hard to be horrible company. Here," he said, lifting a white handkerchief to her eyes.

The small kindness brought another spate of tears, and before Dara knew it his arms were around her and her face was buried in his shoulder.

It hurt to be held by him, hurt her heart, her throat, and she couldn't seem to find a way to shore up her defenses. She pulled away and looked up at him. "Don't be nice," she whispered. "You're making it worse."

He stared at her, confounded. Then he narrowed his eyes and his mouth twisted in irony. "I guess this is one of those situations when it helps to be a crude bastard type. Okay. You were an idiot to get involved in this tonight. It was a kamikaze mission. You need to get tough and say no. And you've ruined my handkerchief.'' Clearly exasperated, he rubbed his hand over the back of his neck. "Hell, Dara, I'm running out of insults, and I feel like I'm kicking a puppy."

At a loss, Dara took a careful breath and struggled to read him.

"Look," he said, picking up her hand. "That poem got to me, too, and compared to you, I've got the hide of a rhinoceros."

Dara felt an easing inside her, as fluid as springwater. All the fussing, hand-holding and the wine were his version of human empathy. She exhaled on a long breath. "So you understand?"

"Yeah. I think I do," he said in a deep, intimate voice that made her heart twist.

"Thank you," she murmured. Feeling the heat of his gaze, she wanted to touch his rough jaw and press her fingers to his lips. She wanted to feel his lips on hers.

The connection clicked between them again with a strength that almost sent her into his arms. She started to move, but a tiny voice of uncertainty rang in her heart. She had, after all, misread him before. "I didn't know bodyguards were all that concerned about the emotional well-being of their clients," she said to remind him and especially herself of the boundaries he'd drawn. She braced herself for his retreat, fully expecting him to pull back.

Denial and frustration, tenderness and passion warred for dominion across his face. "Maybe not." His eyes full of turbulence, he surprised her again and pulled her against him. "But someone's got to make sure you don't run yourself into the ground."

Seven

Dara stiffened, but didn't pull away. "You're being nice again," she muttered.

Ridge resisted the urge to run his hands through the silk of her hair and shifted her head on his shoulder. "Tough. I'm fresh out of crude bastard remarks."

Too tired to argue, she sighed. The darkness of the limo surrounded them like a blanket, the engine provided a soothing hum. "I'm scared," she confessed in a low voice.

Ridge instinctively tightened his arms around her. "There's nothing to be scared of. You know I'm going to protect you. No one will get to you."

He felt her head turn from side to side against his chest. "I'm not scared of getting hurt. I'm scared of letting him down."

Him. A bitter taste rose in Ridge's mouth. "Montgomery."

"Yes. He's done so much for me."

He heard the sincerity in her voice and tamped down a shot of anger. Ridge suspected that despite all the press about what a great godfather Harrison had been, Dara had more than paid the old man back. "And you haven't done anything for him?"

She hesitated. "Not much."

Ridge glanced down to see her cover a yawn. Despite her stressed state, or perhaps because of it, she was fighting sleep. He should probably just shut his mouth and let her drift off, but that choice didn't sit well. He couldn't let her keep believing that about herself. "You haven't worked like a dog for the last year, put in sixty-hour weeks, given up your friends and your privacy."

"Maybe," she agreed reluctantly. "But it's temporary. Besides, I've been paid."

"Yeah, well, so has Montgomery. He's gotten the equivalent of PR gold with you."

She sighed again. Her eyelids fluttered; she was losing the war with drowsiness. "You don't understand. He was the one person who didn't let me down when I was a little girl." Her voice softened. "I don't want to let him down now."

Ridge's gut tightened. He remembered what it was like to be a child who needed someone to depend on. He'd managed on crumbs of stability offered by his grandmother. Even though he hated Harrison Montgomery, part of him was grateful the SOB had done right by Dara. Dara didn't seem to understand, however, that she'd filled a hole in Montgomery's life—that of the child he'd never known.

In effect, Dara had taken what would have been Ridge's rightful place. Resentment ate at him like acid. Knowing all he did about Dara, Ridge couldn't find it in him to resent her for her part in it. He could, however, lay every bit of responsibility at Montgomery's feet. "Montgomery didn't exactly get the short end of the stick," he muttered.

"He sure as hell couldn't have minded having a little girl who worshiped the ground he walked on."

A long silence followed and when Dara didn't dispute him, Ridge shifted and saw that she'd fallen asleep. Sweet and trusting, she curled against Ridge. Her breath puffed gently against his chest.

His heart twisted painfully, and Ridge stared at her. Why did it feel so right to hold her when he knew it was wrong?

Her eyelashes rested like black fans on her cheeks, her lips parted slightly as if she waited for his kiss.

One of her palms fell to his thigh. Ridge felt his muscles tauten immediately. With renewed strength, the desire he constantly battled to control rumbled through him. He wanted to taste her mouth, her throat, her breasts. Hell, he wanted to put his mouth on every forbidden, silken inch of her body. He wanted her to put her generous, provocative mouth on every inch of his body. And then he wanted to be inside her and watch her eyes while he filled her.

Ridge wanted possession.

Just once, he'd like to know her in every possible way. Just once, he'd like to know what it felt like to have her undivided attention and passion.

Just once would be enough, he thought, and gave in to the urge to slide his fingers through her hair.

Just once, he told himself, inhaling her scent. Or twice.

Long after they reached Dara's home and Ridge went to bed, the force of his feelings for Dara filled his mind and dreams. Accustomed to complete control over his thoughts and emotions, Ridge was frustrated enough to punch his hand through the wall. Instead, he got up and ran five miles on the treadmill, then put his body through a punishing weight-lifting routine in the exercise room.

By the next afternoon, at another outdoor rally in Richmond, Ridge had himself back under control. As he

watched the crowd, he was acutely aware of the fact that
Dara had been hit by a bottle at a similar event. This time,
at least, he would have assistance from local law enforcement. Scrutinizing a group of young men with shaved
heads wearing identical T-shirts espousing one of their
group's slogans, Ridge discreetly waved Ray up near the
podium with Dara.

At Dara's introduction, the crowd responded with warm
applause and wolf whistles. She began to speak and in one
corner of his mind, Ridge heard every fervent word of her
speech. Without looking at her, he knew just how the
breeze would be tossing her silky dark hair, and how she
would squint into the crowd searching for a friendly or
familiar face. She'd once told him that seeing a friendly
face helped calm her nerves. He could describe what she
was wearing from the black piping on her red suit with
gold nickel buttons to her black stockings and black
pumps. He wondered if her underwear was black, too. He
would have traded his sanity for the right to find out.

He knew, however, that he wouldn't ever have the right.
His only right was protecting her. She might very well
condemn him to hell after he settled the score with Montgomery, he realized. Ruthlessly, he crushed a twinge of
regret. He could live with that, he told himself, as long as
she was safe.

His gaze skimmed over the restless group of young men.
One of them stretched and Ridge caught sight of a suspi-
cious lump at the back of his waist. He gestured for one of
the police officers and tapped the guy on the shoulder.

"Yeah?" the youth said with a scowl. "What do you
want?"

"Have you got a license to carry that piece?" Ridge
asked, and when the young man's hand wandered to his
back, Ridge shook his head. "I wouldn't even think about
touching it, right now."

"Hey, I gotta right to bear arms. I've got this for pro-tection. This is America. Who the hell are you, anyway? The local gun control lobby?"

"Something like that. I'm here to make sure boys like you don't disrupt the party. You might have a right to bear arms, but you need a license to conceal." Ridge smiled and relieved him of his gun. "But you don't have to talk with me. You can chat with the nice officer, here."

The youth cut loose with a loud string of obscenities that had several people turning to stare. Ridge heard Dara falter. When the young man didn't stop, Ridge clutched his shirt and gave a hard jerk. *"Shut up!"* he whispered tersely.

The youth gave a shrug. "Free speech."

"You can have your turn later." Ridge urged him to-ward the policeman and passed over the weapon.

Scowling, the youth tossed Ridge another resentful glance. "I'm getting my turn. You can count on it. Har-rison Montgomery won't be president if I have anything to say about it."

As the policeman led the offensive youth away, Ridge shot a quick glance at Dara. She looked shaken. Ridge sensed her apprehension twenty feet away. His first in-stinct was to get her off the platform and lock her away from any threat. It cost him, but he resisted. Instead, he put his fist under his chin and nodded, giving her the sign they'd come up with for "chin up."

He could almost feel the deep breath she took in his own tightened chest. She gave the crowd a brave smile and be-gan to speak again. And Ridge sank a little deeper under her spell.

After the rally Dara visited her mother at the residential treatment center where for the last few years she'd spent most of her time. Dara tried her best not to think about the angry young man at the rally, but the ugly reality haunted her. The man had carried a gun. She pushed the event to the back of her mind and concentrated on her mother, then during the drive home, she used the time in the limo to collect her thoughts.

Walking with Ridge through the doorway, she couldn't help remembering his gentleness the night before. He confused her, and Dara didn't have the energy for that brand of confusion. She wanted to snap her fingers and dismiss him from her list of people who mattered to her. She wanted to wave her hand and make her heart pump at its regular rate when he looked at her instead of feeling it pound so hard she felt it in her toes. She wanted to sing a chant that would make her not look at him, not depend on him and most importantly, not want him.

Dara wryly recalled that when she was five years old, she'd also wanted to fly.

"How did the visit go?" Ridge asked.

She shrugged. "She knew who I was, but didn't remember much else."

He followed her into the sunken den. "Is there anything they can do for her?"

"They're doing it. The disease is progressive," she said, drawing strength from hard-won acceptance of her mother's disease. She sank onto the chintz sofa and kicked off her shoes. She had always preferred this room. Through the years, the decor had changed, but the warm, comfortable mood remained, along with her father's antique billiard table. The fire in the fireplace helped her relax.

Studying her, Ridge leaned against the doorjamb. "How long has she lived at the residential center?"

"Five years year-round. She was in and out for a long time before that. I was in fourth grade during her first stay, and it was pretty scary." Dara remembered the sickening fear of watching her mother leave in an ambulance. "I knew something was wrong, and I was afraid of what would happen to me if she had to go away forever. Our housekeeper, Rainy, helped a lot, though. Every Friday she took me to a park in town where I would swing for hours. Afterward, she bought me a snow cone." Dara laughed softly. "I always picked grape and Rainy would scold me for my purple mustache."

Feeling a sudden surge of self-consciousness under Ridge's scrutiny, Dara stopped. Something between them seemed to have shifted since last night. Something that allowed him to ask questions and compelled her to answer. She wondered what it meant. She wondered if she was imagining the whole thing. "You got a whole history lesson with that question," she said with forced lightness, and stood. "I'm getting a soft drink. Do you want one?"

"Yeah. Thanks."

She felt him move closer and frowned at his effect on her nerve endings. The ice cubes clinked loudly in the glasses. The fizz from the soda reflected the sensation in her stomach. She handed Ridge his drink and, disturbed by the too full silence between them, Dara said what had been on her mind since the rally. "That man at the rally. He had a gun."

Ridge's face shifted from thoughtful to cool control. "Yes, he did."

She took a quick sip and jiggled her glass. "Do you think he intended to use it?"

"Not today."

Panic swelled in her chest. Her heart tightened and she sucked in a quick breath. She set her glass down on the wooden bar. "We need to tell Harrison. I should call—"

"I've already talked to Drew. They were in Texas today." His mouth set in a firm line. "After much discussion, it was decided that you will limit your time on the podium for your outdoor rallies. You'll have to trim your speeches down to seven minutes, and we'll be getting more local law enforcement to screen the crowds."

She raised her eyebrows at his tone. He was obviously not pleased. "You don't sound as if you approve."

"I recommended canceling all your outdoor appearances, but Drew said that would be overreacting."

Absently touching the scar on her forehead, Dara reasoned her way past a quick stab of fear. The man hadn't tried to use his gun. He was young and probably just showing off for his friends, she told herself. Election day would be here in a couple of weeks and she didn't want to break Harrison's momentum. "I agree. I've only got a few more outdoor appearances. This was probably just a fluke."

Ridge dipped his head and graced her with a cynical twist of his lips. "That was exactly what Drew said. Everything is secondary to the campaign."

"I didn't say *everything* was."

"But your safety is," he said emphatically.

"Hardly." Dara exhaled in exasperation. "With a slew of police officers, you and Ray taking care of things, I think my safety is pretty much assured. I don't want to wimp out at this stage of the game. It's almost over. Besides, I really don't think you'd—" Breaking off before she revealed too much, she turned away and faced the bar.

"I what?" He moved closer.

She wished he were on the other side of the room, but she had to answer the challenge in his voice. She made herself turn back around and face him. "I really don't think you'd let me get hurt. You're so incredibly bullheaded about my protection that I think you would tell Drew to take a flying leap if you genuinely believed I would be in danger."

"I did make a few suggestions to Drew. He's got a one-track mind that leads straight to the White House. When it comes to your protection, the man is completely ignorant. I don't try to tell him how to do his PR crap, and I sure as hell don't like him telling me how to do my job."

"Oh, and you don't have a one-track mind? I can hardly get a take-out burger without you growling about precautions."

"That's my job," he said through gritted teeth.

"Well, you don't have to be so damn hostile about it." Dara shook her head. "Sometimes I think you would like to lock me in a room with..."

Ridge's unusual eyes locked onto hers with the force of a heat-seeking missile. He didn't say a word. He didn't have to. Yet she knew what he was thinking.

Her own mind shifted to images of being locked in a room with Ridge. The heat in her instantly transformed from anger to something more dangerous—and futile. "Oh, just forget it," she muttered.

"Uh-uh." His hands on his hips, one hip cocked forward, he stood, all male challenge with a touch of anger and a boatload of sensuality. "Finish the sentence. Ridge would like to lock me in a room with..."

At this moment she could really hate him. If there was a fantasy at work in this situation, it was Dara's. She'd like to lock Ridge in a room with her and get rid of this terrible ache, this horrible wanting. She'd rather eat nails than tell him. She lifted her chin. "Bread and water."

He laughed, and the sound vibrated in her stomach. "You don't believe that."

Dara edged slightly away. "Of course I do. You're the one who's into deprivation."

She blinked and his hand was around her wrist, his face mere inches from hers. The intensity of his leonine eyes searching hers made her tremble. "You don't believe that, either," he said quietly, his voice full of sincerity.

Her throat knotted. "I don't have any reason to believe anything else," she whispered.

He shook his head. "What happened between us in New York?"

"You said it was a mistake. The proximity got to us."
She swallowed past the crushing pain and humiliation and
threw his words back at him. "Don't you remember? It
was my swimsuit. It wasn't *me*."

He swore. "I had to keep a clear head." The way he said
it sounded as if it were a mantra he repeated over and over
to himself. "I need to keep my guard up."

"I need to keep my guard up, too," she said desperately.

She tried to pull away, but Ridge held her with his hands
and gaze. "I had to say those things. I had to make some
distance between us."

She felt like a rubber band pulled to the point of snap-
ping. "So what are you trying to tell me, Ridge? That it
was more than my bathing suit? That I might just matter
to you?"

"Yeah, you matter," he said in a deep voice that made
her knees turn to jelly. "But there are reasons—"

Dara's soaring heart took a nosedive. "Because you're
my bodyguard, you can't get emotionally involved."

"That's part of it. I wish it were that simple."

Completely confused, Dara shook her head. "Then
what? Are you married? Engaged? What—"

"There's no one else," he cut in, his eyes turbulent with
emotion. "But there is another reason why it wouldn't
work out between us."

"What?"

He chest rose on a deep breath. "I can't tell you."

"Ohh-hh!" Dara felt like exploding. "You're not being fair!"

He leaned closer to her. A muscle ticked in his jaw.
"Baby, this whole situation isn't fair. Do you think it's fair
that I spend every night dreaming about you in my bed?
Do you think it's fair that I've got to keep my hands off

you day-in and day-out when every time I look at you I remember what you felt like, what you smelled like, what you tasted like. And that night in New York, we weren't finished by a long shot, Dara. Not by a long shot.''

Dara didn't know whether to scream, cry, or beg. She bit her lip and looked away. ''So why bother to tell me? If there's a reason you can't be with me, then why tell me that you care?''

The silence hung heavy and anguished between them. ''Maybe I'm not the super-bodyguard you think I am.''

Dara jerked her head up to meet his eyes.

''I'm not happy with the state of affairs,'' he said in a dark, humorless voice. She felt his gaze on her mouth. ''Or the lack of them.'' He narrowed his eyes and the muscle in his jaw began to tick again. ''I wish—'' he began, and shook his head. ''Hell, I don't even believe in making wishes.''

Dara could barely breathe. He sounded as tied up in knots as she was. ''So what do we do now?''

He almost grinned. Dara saw the faintest flicker, but the taut muscles on his face just wouldn't seem to allow it. ''We stop pretending that we hate each other. You do your campaign work. I watch out for you.''

''And?''

''And I go quietly insane.''

Dara drew little comfort from his confession. She now had intimate knowledge of the word frustration. ''Can I come, too?''

Eight

"**I**'d like to stop by a Mexican restaurant on the way to the Ronald McDonald House party today," Dara announced as she breezed into the den Saturday morning. A study in contrasts, she wore her dark hair clipped back in a ponytail, a white ruffled shirt, black jeans, and knee socks with no shoes in sight yet. Her face devoid of makeup, she looked at him with clear blue eyes that emanated a feminine strength Ridge hadn't glimpsed since he'd first met her.

He sensed something different about her, as if she had reluctantly obliged Ridge's determination to resist an involvement at the same time *she* decided to stop denying her own attraction for him. His body responded immediately, and the term that came to mind was *dangerous*.

He'd thought that if he put their mutual attraction out in the open, they'd be able to handle it better. Now he wasn't so sure. If God had created a woman to be Ridge's waterloo, she would be Dara. When his fingers itched to release the pearl buttons of her blouse, he reminded himself that they had no future. And just because he had an arousal that wouldn't quit didn't mean he would let her get away with skipping security measures. He lifted his eyebrows. "Ronald McDonald House party?"

"Oops," Dara said, with a wince that quickly spread to a smile. "I guess I forgot to tell you last night."

"According to your itinerary," Ridge reminded her firmly, "you're going to a fund-raiser tonight."

"Right." She nodded. "And this afternoon I'm going to a party," she said just as firmly.

"I like advance notice."

Her expressive face flashed with impatience. "I would have told you, but the person in charge called yesterday morning. I didn't get a chance to tell you last night because we were talking about other things."

He didn't respond to her meaningful comment about "other things." After she'd gone to bed last night, he'd spent more than an hour on the back porch struggling to keep his perspective on Dara from being shot to hell. Ridge sighed, contemplating the different precautions he would need to take. "When you make a schedule change that will involve security, you need to let me know as soon as possible."

"This is as soon as possible. And you don't have to come if you don't want to."

Ridge narrowed his eyes. "I go everywhere you go."

She opened her mouth to make a heated reply, then paused. A soft feminine chuckle bubbled out instead. Giving him a sideways glance rife with seduction, she shook her head. "Everywhere I go?" She held his gaze and her voice grew husky. "I wish."

Ridge stifled a groan at the blatant sexual invitation in her voice. "You're not making it easy for either of us when you say things like that."

"Making it easy wasn't part of our little agreement. Let me know if you change your mind," she told him, bold as brass.

"Dara," he began, his voice full of warning.

Reluctantly heeding his wishes, she sighed. "Okay, okay," she grumbled. "The party's from two to four, and I won't be at the Mexican restaurant more than five minutes." She flicked a glance over his casual attire. "You don't need to change."

"Thank you," he said in a mocking tone.

By three-thirty, Dara was seated with twelve children in front of a television set that played Speedy Gonzales videos at the Ronald McDonald House. All, including Dara, wore wide-brimmed sombreros and chorused along with Speedy's *¡Arriba! ¡Andale!*

Dara glanced over her shoulder at Ridge, and scooting back from the children, she beckoned him closer. "Put on a hat and come up here with us. Everyone except you has worn one." She lowered her voice. "Even that stuffy social reporter."

Ridge swallowed back his amusement. Dara had charmed everyone into putting on the ridiculous headwear. "The brim would inhibit my peripheral vision."

"Peripheral vision of what? The closest thing to a weapon around this place is a super-soaker water gun."

He shook his head. "I've got to watch the doors."

Dara rolled her eyes. "Are all bodyguards this anal retentive?"

"Just the good ones," he told her smugly, and tugged the hat over her eyes.

"Someday," she muttered, pushing back the hat and glaring at him. "I'm going to—" She broke off midthreat when a little girl pulled on her arm and told her she was missing Speedy. Dara gave the little girl a hug, but obviously couldn't resist one last dig at Ridge. "I'm saving one of these hats for you, and you'll wear it by election day."

"No chance," he said succinctly, and resisting the urge to kiss her impudent mouth, he returned to his place in the hall. God, he liked sparring with her. He liked it that she was comfortable enough with him that she felt she could joke, but it sure as hell didn't create the much-needed distance between them. She oozed a come-and-get-me attitude that made her teasing like torturous foreplay.

The director, Liz Clayton, held her own hat and chuckled. "When Miss Seabrook asked what she could bring and I suggested hats, I never expected this."

Ridge nodded, glancing at the kids' animated faces. It didn't take a genius to understand the request. Several of the children were receiving chemotherapy and had begun to lose their hair. "You have these parties every month."

"Absolutely. It was a real coup to get Miss Seabrook to attend."

"You mean, the press coverage," he said, referring to the reporters who'd left only moments before.

"We rely on private donations, so every bit of exposure helps, and it's true that the press has been tracking nearly every move Miss Seabrook has made." She gave Drew a speculative glance. "I'm sure it's difficult for her personal relationships."

Ridge neither confirmed nor denied the woman's statement. It bothered him that everyone seemed to want a piece of Dara, yet didn't comprehend that she needed a break.

The director sighed. "The kids love her."

His gut twisted. In the most hidden part of his mind, Ridge snapped and sealed the picture of Dara in a sombrero, her arms around children on either side of her, and another one in her lap. She'd left her designer dress, heels, and careful smile at home.

She made him laugh, she made him burn, but most of all, she made him care and feel. She was everything he'd ever wanted, he realized.

He thought of Harrison Montgomery and wished like hell Dara had no connection with the man. Dissatisfaction pumped through him with every beat of his heart. A gnawing emptiness yawned deep inside him, but the truth remained.

She was everything he'd ever wanted.

But couldn't have.

That evening at the banquet it took twice as much effort for Dara to concentrate on the dinner conversation swirling around her. One man remarked on the recent abysmal performance of the Washington Redskins football team. Another was shaking his head over the Democratic majority in the senate while his wife complimented Dara on her dress.

Despite her mood, Dara smiled and responded to each person. Inside, she was steaming. Not because the fall temperatures had surged into the low sixties and not because she wore blue velvet. She was pissed at Ridge.

She'd thought they'd reached an understanding last night, so she'd invited him to ride in the back of the limo with her to the banquet. He had refused. Just as she was recovering from the sting of his rejection, he'd had the audacity to instruct her to limit her dance partners to men she knew.

While she was sputtering her response, he'd slammed the car door shut. She was so furious she hadn't looked at him since. Although Dara scrupulously avoided juvenile contests of one-upmanship, she was tempted to teach Ridge a lesson he wouldn't forget.

I understand there will be dancing tonight. If you decide to cut the rug, stick with men you know.

Dara stifled the urge to scream by downing a few gulps of ice water. The temptation to teach Ridge a lesson was like an insistent tickle that wouldn't go away. She toyed with an idea, and temptation turned to strategy and determination.

Smiling at the middle-aged lawyer sitting next to her, a man she'd never met before, Dara cocked her head to one side. "This is one of my favorite songs. Would you mind a turn around the dance floor?"

The man sat up a little straighter and smiled in return. "It will be my pleasure."

And so the evening went. She took a fifteen-minute break to eat dinner, sat down during the speech, and took one powder room break, but spent the rest of the time on the dance floor. Despite her unimpressive balance, she fudged her way through the rhumba, the waltz, a country two-step, the cha-cha, and the jitterbug. By the time she was ready to leave, the only thing she hadn't done was the hokey-pokey.

"I'm ready to go," she said blithely to a stone-faced Ridge as she swept past him toward the door.

"This way," he said in a terse voice, directing her toward the limo.

She murmured her thanks when he opened the door. After she got in, she gave a little shrug and smiled sweetly. "Great band."

Ridge slammed the door.

This time, however, the sound was infinitely satisfying.

During the drive home, she slipped out of her shoes and relaxed enough to fall asleep. Waking to find the limo stopped outside her home, she grimaced as she attempted to slide her swollen feet into her shoes. After a few tries she gave up and decided to walk in stocking feet to the front door. It wasn't that far.

Watching the chauffeur walk toward the house, she wondered why he'd left the engine running. She put her hand on the door latch. Ridge's voice sounded over the limo intercom, crisp and authoritative. "Please remain in the car, Miss Seabrook."

Dara arched her eyebrows. *So, we're back to Miss Seabrook.* She snickered. Pressing the button, she asked in her coolest tone, "Why should I, Mr. Jackson?"

Silence followed, and she could practically hear Ridge grind his teeth. "Because we're not quite finished this evening," he said in a deep, super-controlled voice.

"Does this have anything to do with my security?"

"You could say that."

Dara wondered what he meant by that statement. A little frisson of uneasiness shimmied down her spine. It wasn't totally unpleasurable. No matter how angry Ridge was, he wouldn't physically harm her, she assured herself. After all, as he'd told her ad nauseum, he was responsible for her safety and well-being.

When she didn't respond, the car moved forward. Wariness tugging at her, Dara leaned back in her seat, curious to see what he would do next.

After several minutes the car stopped. Dara peered out the window and saw...nothing but a field.

The door opened and Ridge stared down at her. He'd ditched his jacket and tie. His white shirt was augmented by dark suspenders and the sleeves were folded up to his forearms. His shoulders looked impossibly broad, his face, heart-wrenchingly masculine. "You can get out now."

Reluctant, Dara frowned. "Where are we?"

"A field about two miles from your house. It's okay. We're alone."

Something about his you-asked-for-it expression had uneasiness climbing into her throat. "If it's all the same to you, I'll just stay in the car."

Ridge bent closer and stretched out his hand. "It's not all the same to me. Come out."

"Why?"

Ridge gritted his teeth. "To have a quiet discussion," he said. "Or a screaming match that won't be overheard by the housekeeper. Your choice."

Sighing, she crammed her feet into her shoes and stepped out of the car, avoiding his hand. "Okay, okay. I'm out. Now what—"

Ridge slipped his arm around her waist and began to walk. "Did you enjoy yourself tonight?"

She tried to ignore the silky dark tone in his voice. "I guess. Considering what kind of event it was, the evening passed pretty quickly." She took a deep breath and inhaled the scents of hay, fallen leaves, and Ridge's aftershave. Stars winked in the sky. A full moon shed plenty of light on the field. And the soft breeze was divine. If she wasn't nervous, she might actually like this little stroll.

"I didn't realize you enjoyed dancing so much."

Dara smiled. "I was inspired."

"How many of those men did you know?" he asked in a deliberately casual voice.

"Oh, I don't know. Maybe ten."

His hand tightened, then relaxed. "You danced with thirty-four men."

"I wasn't counting."

"I counted because it's my job to notice."

Dara looked up and saw the ticking muscle in his cheek. "Then I'm sure you also noticed that all of my dance partners were perfect gentlemen."

Ridge abruptly stopped. "I told you to stick to men you know. Why in hell did you disregard my instructions?"

"Because you didn't ask nicely."

His face was incredulous. "I— What?"

"You acted like a jerk."

Ridge quickly recovered. "And you're acting like a brat."

"I'm behaving the way any independent woman would." Dara turned back toward the car. "You made a suggestion. I thought about it and disregarded it."

"You were pissed because I wouldn't sit in the limo with you."

She wanted to deny it. She almost did. Instead she rounded on him. "So what if I was?"

Clearly disconcerted, Ridge stared at her.

She pointed a finger at his chest. "*You* said we were going to stop pretending we hated each other. I took you at your word, and politely invited you to join me. You refused. My feelings were hurt. Then you told me not to dance with strangers and slammed the car door in my face."

"I didn't slam the damn door in your face."

Dara crossed her arms over her chest and gave him a look of disbelief.

He swore. "Have you taken a good look at yourself tonight? Do you have any idea how you look? Any idea how that dress looks on you?"

Dropping her arms, Dara looked down at her dress and shrugged. The rich fabric skimmed her curves without being too tight, and ended just above the knee. She had bought it because she had liked the color and the flattering sweetheart neckline. But mostly, she'd loved the way it felt. "The color's nice, but it's no different from what I wear to all these—"

His hand on her cheek stalled her words. He looked at her as if he couldn't bear to not touch her any longer. "The color makes your eyes look like sapphires," he corrected in a rough voice, and brushed his fingers down her neck. "The velvet looks soft." One lone finger skimmed down to the deep V between her breasts. "But your skin looks softer. It shows just enough to drive a man nuts wondering what the rest looks like, what it feels like."

He slid his finger beneath the material and Dara held her breath. When Ridge grazed that terrible, wonderful finger over her nipple, she shuddered. Back and forth, he caressed the beaded tip, drawing a tight string of sensation from her breasts to her womb. The delicate yet persistent touch had her biting back a moan. She reached for his arm.

As if he realized he'd crossed the line, he slowly moved his hand away, and she had to right the urge to ask him to keep touching her. "I can guarantee that every man who held you tonight wanted to take you home and find out what was underneath that dress. There were probably a few who even suggested it."

Dara seriously doubted his first statement although three men had tried to wrangle a quiet get-together after the banquet. Her face must have revealed her thoughts.

Ridge scowled. "Who hit on you?"

Still recovering from Ridge's touch, she waved a dismissive hand. "Nobody I wanted to go home with." She folded her arms over her sensitive breasts and turned away from him. The irony of the romantic setting hit her. She wanted to be close enough to feel his heartbeat, and they were arguing like children. "You know, Ridge, I didn't have to dance with thirty-four men tonight to be happy. I would have been happy just to dance with one."

His hands squeezed her shoulders. She felt his breath on her bare shoulder, his heat at her back, and she wanted more than anything to lean against him. "We can't—" he began.

"Don't tell me what we can and don't do." Struggling with a sense of futility, Dara stared up at the sky. "Don't lecture me about a bodyguard's responsibilities and the mysterious reasons why you can't hold me. Sometimes I think I fight with you because I can't be with you the way I want to. Each time I danced with a man tonight, I wished he was you. I wished it was your hand holding mine, your arms around me. I wished it was you looking at me. I must be an idiot, because I just don't see the sin in you dancing with me."

So frustrated she felt near tears, Dara swallowed over the lump in her throat. "There. That should swell your head to the size of a watermelon and send your ego into the stratosphere.'' He was too close and it was too tempting to turn around and fold herself into his arms. Dara straightened. ''I'm tired. I want to go home.''

She took two steps away and his hand pulled her back around. His gaze burning her with its intensity, he tugged her closer, all the while shaking his head. When she was inches from him, he wrapped his fingers in her hair. ''You have an annoying habit of saying things that tie me into knots,'' he said, full of self-derision. ''I spent this whole night torn between wanting to beat the smile off of every man who danced with you and wringing your neck for being so damn beautiful.''

He took her hand and pressed it to his hard chest. She felt the thump of his heart and the deep breath he took. Her own heart picked up the pace. ''There's no reason for you to be jealous of any of those men.''

''They held you, and I didn't,'' he said roughly, his eyes turbulent.

Your choice. It was on the tip of her tongue to say it, but she didn't. For a moment she could empathize with being pulled in opposing directions. The campaign had taught her how frustrating that could be.

Something shifted in his gaze, and Ridge lifted her left hand to his shoulder. Watching her with his lion's eyes, he curled his hand around hers at his chest while he slowly tugged her closer and closer until her body meshed against his. His muscular thighs rubbed against hers. His arousal branded her stomach. She sucked in a shallow breath.

Cupping his hand around her bottom, he urged her closer still. Then he lowered his head and brushed his mouth against her shoulder. His lips were firm and moist.

Dara felt dizzy. ''What are we doing?''

''We're dancing.'' His tongue darted out to stroke her skin and he gently rocked his pelvis against hers.

Holding on to his shoulder for dear life, Dara instinctively arched against him.

He groaned and shifted his feet to an imaginary tune. He kissed her forehead. "Just a little dance," he promised, his voice not so steady. She pressed her lips to his throat and felt his chest swell beneath her hand.

The moonlight spilled around them, and the yearning surged between them, so tangible she could feel it in her lungs and the force of his heartbeat. He cuddled her against him as if he couldn't possibly bring her close enough, and the beauty of the gesture was almost too much to take. She swallowed hard. It was just a dance. Why did it mean so much?

A kaleidoscope of emotions circled through Dara—too much to try to sort through when she was in Ridge's arms. The rustling of fallen leaves could have been the wind section of an orchestra. Ridge's steady heartbeat was the percussion. And Dara was sure the longing in her heart made the poignant, bittersweet sound of a violin. The music played in her mind. For the moment she closed her eyes and mind to everything but him. It was magic. "Just a little dance," she whispered, letting her feet follow the rhythm of his.

He nuzzled her cheek. "Just a little insanity."

Nine

Everyone was on edge the following morning.

Clarence drummed his fingers on the desk as he waited for a fax from Drew. Not one for chatting, Ray chewed gum and jingled the keys in his pocket as he paced the Oriental rug in front of the fireplace. Ridge clicked his pen as he confirmed arrangements by phone with the local police in West Virginia where the rally would be held.

Fighting off her own tension, Dara gravitated closer to Ridge. Focused on his telephone conversation, he scratched out a few notes on a notepad. He wore a crisp white shirt with the leather gun holster, minus the hated tie. It was beyond her understanding how he could be so comfortable with a gun slung over his shoulder, yet a tie seemed to drive him nuts.

His face was intent, his tone clipped and forceful. She thought wryly that she was glad she wasn't the one on the other end of the line. From head to toe he oozed intimidation, but the effect was softened by the one lock of his dark hair that spilled over his forehead. It made him seem more human. It made her want to touch him.

Dara stretched out a hand to rearrange his hair, then stopped midway. Looking up, Ridge glanced at her hand and his eyes darkened. He crooked his finger for her to sit beside him on the sofa.

Dara allowed her hand to fall to her side. She sat and laced her fingers together in her lap. It was harder not to touch him, especially after last night. She wondered if it was hard for him, or if he was able to compartmentalize his thoughts and emotions. If so, she envied him.

"You okay?" he asked after he hung up the phone.

Dara nodded. "Yes." *But I'd be better if my hands didn't seem to have a mind of their own.*

Ridge gazed at her searchingly. "You sure? You seem a little..."

"Crazy," Dara said in a low voice. "I'm just feeling a little crazy today."

Ridge's chest swelled as he took a deep breath. His concentration wasn't going to be worth spit if she kept this up. "Cut me some slack. I need a clear head today."

She bowed her head and rubbed her forehead, effectively shielding her expression. "Fine. Just tell me I'm not the only one having trouble this morning."

"You're not," he growled.

"Okay."

"Okay." He turned the conversation to business. "The weather's great and the advance publicity has been extensive, so we're expecting a heavy turnout today. We'll arrive about fifteen minutes before you speak. I'll get you onto the platform. Ray gets you off. Then we head back to the limo."

Dara shook her head skeptically. "That doesn't leave much time for shaking hands."

"Yeah, well, we're keeping the handshaking to a minimum with this appearance."

"Is Drew okay with this?"

Ridge really didn't care if it was okay with Drew. "You said it yourself. Drew can take a flying leap."

Her lips slowly stretched into a grin and she opened her mouth to say something, but Clarence distracted her by placing a piece of paper in her lap. "What's this?" she asked.

"A fax from Drew," Clarence said, his expression grim. "Willis Herkner smells fresh meat."

Dara quickly read the letter and shook her head in disgust.

"Who's Willis Herkner?" Ridge asked, wondering why this man upset her.

Dara's eyes flashed. "He goes by the nickname 'Weasel' and writes for one of the rag magazines. If there aren't facts to be found, you can be sure he'll find the most absurd and twisted rumors to print." She didn't bother to hide the anger in her voice as she turned to Clarence. "What does this idiot think he has on Harrison?"

"We don't know, yet," Clarence said. "All Drew said was that they were digging for dirt all the way back to before Harrison was born."

Ridge felt a shadow of dread cross over him.

"I'd love to see him completely discredited. In fact," Dara said in a rare display of outright aggression, "I'd like to be the one to do it."

Ridge struggled with a bitter taste of victory and his diametrically opposed concern for Dara. He wanted Harrison Montgomery's failings exposed for the world to see, but part of him cringed at what that would do to Dara. He flexed his shoulders to relieve his tension. "Do you have any idea what they're looking for?"

Clarence shook his head. "Anything. Anything the weasel can find."

"Will he go after Dara?"

Both Clarence and Dara stared at Ridge.

Clarence made a moue of surprise. "I hadn't thought of that."

"What could he find about me?"

"I don't know," Ridge said, hating the fact that he couldn't protect her from the effects of the tabloids. Headlines flashed through his mind. "Would they go after your mother?"

Dara paled. "They wouldn't dare." Her gaze shot to Clarence. "Would they?"

"Oh, Lord." Clarence squeezed the bridge of his nose. "I suppose they could, but it's really not new news. Your mother has been ill for some time, and it's not as if she ever did anything truly scandalous in public."

"No," Dara murmured, still looking worried. "Not in public. The fact that she lives at the residential center would insulate her. And the people who visit her already know about her illness."

"You might," Clarence said tentatively, "suffer from some of the backlash."

Dara narrowed her eyes, and Ridge sensed a stiffening in her resolve. "Then maybe I'll just have to take that trip to the Caribbean Harrison keeps talking about. After the election," she clarified. "Two weeks away would give me some breathing room, and the tabloids will move on to something else."

His gut tightened at the thought of the end of the campaign. He and Dara would say goodbye. And what had Ridge accomplished? Had he exacted his revenge on Montgomery? He wondered why he vacillated at the notion. Was he going soft?

Ridge searched for the hard kernel of hate for Montgomery that had been inside him so long that it was a part of his identity. Within a second he found it glowing like a hot coal inside him. At the same moment he saw Dara put her arms around herself—a gesture of vulnerability that made his hate for Montgomery fade. Despite her bravado, she was scared. She just didn't want to admit it.

Ridge barely resisted the urge to put his hand over hers to add his strength to hers. "They might not be able to find anything worth printing."

Doubt shimmered in her eyes, but she squared her shoulders. "Maybe not, but if I ever get my hands on Willis the Weasel, I'm nailing him and his polyester pants to the wall."

Clarence wore a woeful expression. "It would be easier to nail jam."

"Yo, lady and gents, it's time to go," Ray interrupted, tossing the limo keys up and catching them. He quirked his mouth in a half grin intended to reassure. "Those mountains are calling your name."

Ray was pumped, Ridge thought. He usually felt the same way on jobs. But not on this one, though, he thought as he looked at Dara. This time, he felt an insidious sense of dread.

After the two-hour drive to West Virginia, the first thing Ridge noticed was that the crowd was nearly double Drew's estimate. A high school band played Montgomery's theme song. Beer and soft drinks flowed freely. With just a few clouds in the sky and the temperatures warmed up to the fifties, the rally resembled a party teetering on the edge of being out of control. Worse still, a group of student pacifists were preaching at a group of Vietnam vets, and an extremist organization was annoying the hell out of everyone. He would have to keep a sharp eye out for trouble.

Struggling with a desire to call the whole thing off, Ridge scowled and opened Dara's door instead.

She glanced at him as she stepped from the limo wearing an electric blue suit that reminded him of the blue velvet she'd worn the night before. Funny how both of them suited her personality. The velvet was soft and romantic, the suit was classic with a kick.

"What's wrong? You look like you could chew glass."

"No," Ridge muttered. "I'd just like to wrap Drew's tongue around his throat." He nodded at a few of the policemen, then said to Dara, "Remember. Seven minutes on the stage. Don't get long-winded."

"I'm never long-winded," she said with a huff.

Ridge nearly grinned at the tone of her voice. "Right. Don't get too friendly afterward, either. Clarence contacted the local people, and they'll convey your regrets that you can't hang around. Ray will bring you behind the platform, and we'll walk you back to the car."

"You've thought of everything." She touched his sunglasses. "Is this standard equipment for Secret Service and bodyguard types?"

Ridge did grin that time. She was obviously trying to get him to lighten up. "Yeah."

"The mirrored lenses are so clear I could probably put on lipstick looking into them."

A purely hedonistic, lustful thought crossed his mind, but Ridge didn't share it.

Dara cocked her head thoughtfully to one side, her bangs sweeping over one eye. "Say it out loud."

"What?" he asked, surprised that she read him so easily.

"What you were thinking." She stepped closer and her scent swam around him. "Say it out loud."

Well, hell. Something inside him wouldn't allow him to back away from the challenge in her voice. "I was thinking of a few creative ways of taking off that lipstick after you put it on."

Her eyes darkened to indigo. "There's a name for men like you," she said, and started walking toward the platform.

Ridge immediately caught up to her side and kept one eye on the crowd. "What's that?"

"It's the same one for women." She tossed her hair and pursed her lips in the kind of pout designed to send a man's blood pressure into the ozone. Ridge wasn't the least bit immune.

"Tease," she whispered in a silky voice. "You know, somebody who promises, but doesn't deliver."

Then, as she turned away from him, she smiled at the official extending his hand to her from the steps of the platform, and left Ridge watching her incredible derriere and wanting to teach her a lesson about exactly what he'd like to deliver.

Her speech lasted six minutes and fifty-eight seconds. Ridge felt Dara's glance at him, and he gave a chiding shake of his head. Always pushing it, she gave him a blinding smile and winked.

The crowd applauded enthusiastically as she descended the platform steps. After he made sure Ray was waiting for her, Ridge swept his gaze over the horde of constituents. Despite the mayor's announcement that Dara would leave early, a large group of people surged in her direction.

He tensed, hoping Ray had the sense to move her along quickly. Glancing over, Ridge saw Ray attempting to do just that. However, a little girl was presenting Dara with two rosebuds. Dara bent down and kissed the little girl on the cheek, then smiled as the youngster skipped away.

To Dara's immediate right, a man from the extremist group began scuffling with another man in the crowd. A third man got involved, and all hell broke loose. Ridge ran toward Dara at the same time he saw Ray take a punch. Pushing the unruly crowd aside, he saw Dara go down and felt his heart fall to his feet.

The people were crammed together so tightly, he might as well have been trying to part the Red Sea. It couldn't have been five seconds, but it felt like hours before he reached her, pulling her up from the ground and holding her against his chest. Dimly aware of a high heel spiking into his ankle and an elbow in his ribs, he forged a pathway out of the mayhem.

His lungs felt swollen to the size of basketballs by the time he chanced a glance at Dara. A bruise already coloring her cheekbone, the shoulder of her suit torn and stained, she stared up at him shell-shocked. "Ray! He's still—" She gulped. "Ray, we need to—"

Ridge shook his head. The woman had nearly been stampeded and she was worried about someone else. "Hush. Let me get you to the limo first."

Police sirens screamed as Ridge jerked the car door open and placed her inside. Clarence came running from his own car. He'd driven himself because he'd planned to stay longer than Dara. "Oh, my God, is she all right?"

"I don't know. She might be in shock." His body and mind pumped with adrenaline, he tore off his sport coat and wrapped it around her. "What hurts?"

She shrugged helplessly. "I don't know," she said in an unsteady voice, lifting a hand to her face and wincing. "My cheek." She wiggled her arms and legs. "My shoulder feels a little sore, but I think I'm okay."

His stomach tightened at the sight of her. She looked so pale and frightened. "We need to get you out of here *now*."

"No." Dara grabbed his hand with icy fingers. "You've got to go get Ray. What if he got—" her face crumpled "—trampled because he was trying to protect me?"

Hell! Ridge deliberately kept his voice low and gentle. "That's his job—to protect you. I don't want to see him hurt any more than you do, but the first priority here has got to be you. Ray—"

"No!" Dara squeezed his hand desperately and began to tremble. "I'm fine. You've got to go back and get Ray."

Losing a fraction of his ominous self-control, Ridge let
out a litany of oaths that rendered Dara mute and had
Clarence's eyes bulging. "You have got to trust me,"
Ridge said in a harsh voice.

Biting her lip, Dara squinted her eyes, clearly fighting
tears. "This is all my fault. If I hadn't stopped for that little girl, it wouldn't have happened."

If he didn't feel so sorry for her Ridge would have
shaken her. "You're wrong."

Her face tightening mutinously, she met his gaze. "Find
Ray."

Hell. Ridge rubbed the back of his neck in complete
frustration. She was asking him to break a cardinal rule.
A bodyguard never lets his client out of sight. *Never. Ever.*

Ambulance sirens now mingled with the police sirens,
and someone was shouting directions from the loudspeaker. Ridge glanced over the crowd, which seemed to
be quickly breaking up. He looked back at Dara, wanting
more than anything to get her the hell out of here.

She took a deep, shuddery breath. "Please."

"Okay, okay," he grumbled. "Clarence you stay with
her until I get back. Keep the doors locked. Yell at the first
sign of trouble."

Clarence nodded, Ridge slammed the door, and jogged
past the platform. Ray was already being attended to by a
member of the emergency medical team. Ridge bent down
to speak to the battered man. "You okay?"

Ray shrugged. "Just a few scratches. I might have a
couple of cracked ribs, so they want to take me to the hospital." His face shifted in concern. "What about Dara? I
tried to get her out of there, but I swear that fight must
have started when I blinked."

Ridge nodded. "I got her out. She's a little shaken up,
but I think she'll be all right. She was mostly concerned
about you."

Ray winced as he shifted his weight. "That sounds like her." He shooed Ridge away. "Go ahead. Tell her I'm fine, and get outta here."

That mission accomplished, he snagged an EMT on his return to the limo and got Dara checked out. No serious injuries, the woman confirmed, and gave Dara an icepack to hold on her cheek.

Ridge drove out of the field and spent the entire ride replaying the whole scene in his mind. It became a torturous game of answering the questions 'How could I have handled it differently? What should I have done to protect Dara better?' Subjecting his decisions to a ruthless but necessary analysis, he studied the incident from every angle.

His stomach turned at the image of Dara's eyes wide with fear. His mouth filled with a bitter taste at the realization that it could have been worse. That bruise on her cheek was enough to make him want to kill someone. When he thought about that horrible moment when she'd fallen from his sight, he realized his objectivity was shot. He shuddered to think how he would react if her injuries were more serious.

Although he didn't blame Drew for Dara's accident, by the time Ridge pulled into Dara's driveway, he'd made a firm decision. No more outdoor rallies for Dara. Drew and anyone else could go straight to hell if they thought anything different.

Despite Dara's protest, Ridge arranged for a doctor to come by and examine her one more time. Clarence sent out press releases and fielded questions from inquisitive reporters. Fussing over everyone, especially Dara, Rainy served homemade soup and sandwiches.

The phone rang about three hours after they had returned. It was Drew.

"How is she?" he asked.

Ridge explained her minor injuries, then added, "She's a little shaken up."

"What happened?"

Although he'd expected it, Ridge didn't like the accusing tone in Drew's voice. "The crowd was double your estimate. We could have used more guards, but we would have needed an army to prepare for the extremist group."

Drew swore. "This is a public relations nightmare."

"That's your game, not mine," he said without an ounce of sympathy.

"How shaken up is she? Maybe she could make an appearance this afternoon or tomorrow to reassure the press. How bad is her cheek? Do you think she could cover it up?"

Ridge was completely disgusted. "She's not doing anything for twenty-four hours. Even the doctor said she should rest. As for her bruise, it looks like it's gonna hurt like hell, not that you'd be concerned about a little thing like Dara's comfort."

"I resent your sarcasm, Jackson. I've got a job to do and you're—"

"Yeah, well. You haven't exactly made mine a walk through the garden."

Drew sighed in exasperation. "Maybe I should talk to her."

"She's asleep," Ridge said flatly.

"When she wakes up, have her call me. I want to talk to her. I need to determine how much this has rattled her and if she can..." Drew paused as if he finally realized how callous he sounded.

"If she can still do the job, or if she won't be useful to you and Montgomery anymore," Ridge said in a low, furious voice.

"I didn't say that."

Ridge shook his head. "You didn't have to. I gotta go. I'll tell Dara you—"

"Wait." Drew's breath was audible. "We need to go over the plans for her last two outdoor rallies."

Ridge counted to ten. "Dara isn't doing anymore outdoor rallies."

"Oh, come on. We've discussed this before."

"That was then. This is now. As of twelve-thirty this afternoon, Dara Seabrook's appearances at her remaining two outdoor rallies have been canceled."

Drew sputtered with outrage. "You—you took that action without my approval?"

"I did."

Dead silence followed. "When Harrison hears about this, your ass will be out the door so fast you'll—"

"Fine," Ridge interrupted calmly. "Have him call. I'm through talking with you." Then Ridge hung up on Drew Forrester, the act filling him with enormous satisfaction.

He was just taking a bite out of one of Rainy's sandwiches when the phone rang again thirty minutes later. This time it was Harrison Montgomery. Ridge's appetite disappeared.

"About this afternoon . . ." Montgomery began.

Ridge didn't even let the man finish. "You want my ass out the door, then that's fine, but I'm not letting Dara appear at any more outdoor rallies. She's the only one campaigning for you who has been hurt. You hired me to prevent that, and I'll be damned if it happens again."

Silence followed, then Montgomery cleared his throat. "I was calling to apologize for my public relations director's behavior. If you believe any of her scheduled appearances will place her in danger, then you must cancel," he said firmly and then sighed.

"Dara has a rare quality of making magic with the camera. People are captivated by her pictures. When they find out how approachable she is in person, they want to get closer. I'll be the first to say she's brought our ticket an incredible amount of positive media coverage. But I can't have her suffering because of the campaign.''

Ridge couldn't have spoken if his life depended on it. *Montgomery concerned about someone besides himself? Was it possible?* Bitterness lodged in his chest. Ridge had been certain that for Montgomery nothing was more important than winning the presidency.

"I understand she's asleep," Montgomery continued, his voice showing the edge of weariness. "I hear her injuries are not too serious, but how is she?''

"Shaky," Ridge told him. "I think she'll be back to herself tomorrow, and if not, the day after.''

The older man sighed, and Ridge heard a wealth of relief in the sound. "I'd like to hear from her when she wakes in the morning.''

"I'll tell her.''

"Take care of her." The sound of command returned to Montgomery's voice.

Ridge didn't pause. "I will," he said and realized he'd accomplished part of his plan. Montgomery trusted him.

The realization wasn't nearly as satisfying as Ridge had expected.

Ten

It was just for ninety minutes, Dara told herself as she strolled through the quiet park of her childhood days. Rain clouds threatened, and the temperature had taken a dip, but Dara was so relieved to escape she would have walked through a blizzard.

She refused to consider how Ridge would react if he found out. Since the rally, she was sure she'd been watched nearly every minute, including the hours when she'd slept. Forced to present a calm front to reassure everyone, she felt like a boiling pot ready to explode.

Just a little quiet, she'd told Rainy. *Just a little time to myself.* It took some persuasion, but the housekeeper agreed to cover for Dara.

Spying the swings, she pulled her denim jacket closer around her and walked toward them. Sitting in the moldable rubber seat, she wryly concluded that these were obviously designed for ten-year-old kids.

Despite the discomfort, she remained, twisting around in a circle and digging the toe of her tennis shoe in the dirty sand as she tried to find a shred of inner peace. She must have sat there fifteen minutes before the sound of footsteps rustling through the leaves caught her attention. It amazed her how his shadow managed to loom over her despite the stingy sunlight.

She didn't need to look up to determine the identity of the intruder. "Have a seat," she said, gesturing toward the swing beside her.

Ridge paused, then settled into the swing, and Dara caught the tense, guarded expression on his face. "You left without telling me."

Dara nodded. "Yes, I did. I needed to be by myself for a while. Everyone was ... hovering."

"I could have arranged—"

"No," Dara interrupted, feeling her stomach knot. She stood. "You might have arranged for me to get out, but you would have been hovering like a good bodyguard should. And I didn't need a bodyguard. I needed a friend," she said quietly. "Or nobody at all."

She jammed her hands into her pockets and turned slowly away. She heard the squeak of the rusty chain as he left his swing and stepped to her side.

He tugged her arm so that she faced him and his gaze searched hers. "I don't want to play games with you today," he said, low and quiet. "You've been through a lot, and I'm worried about you."

His words sent a quivering deep within her. That boiling pot of emotions flared up again. Her body leaned toward his and of its own accord. More needy than bold, she asked, "How do you feel about holding me?"

His eyes darkened, and across his face she could see him struggle between resistance and need. His hesitation lasted one beat too long for her fragile reserve. She took a quick breath and turned away.

No sooner had she turned than she found herself in his arms, her back against his chest. "You don't give a guy much time to think it over, do you?" he growled.

Swiveling in his arms, she pressed her face to his throat and inhaled the scent of his leather jacket and after-shave. He was big and solid and warm, his masculine strength irresistible. She stretched her hands around his back.

When she didn't say anything, he sifted his fingers through her hair. "You have an annoying habit—"

"Another one?" Dara smiled against his skin. Lord, he felt good.

He gave her a squeeze. "Of doing the unexpected."

"My godfather says it's one of my charms."

Ridge softly cursed. "He would. Did you talk to him this morning?"

She backed slightly away and nodded. "He made noises about flying in to see me, but I reminded him about the luncheon we'll both be attending the day before the election." She felt Ridge's body stiffen and sighed. "I wish you didn't dislike him."

"I dislike politics."

"Harrison isn't all bad. If he hadn't pulled my father out of a trap in Vietnam, I wouldn't be here today." She felt the bittersweet remnant of grief for never having known her father. "They became close friends. People say Harrison was never the same after my father died years later." She saw the grim expression on his face and pinched him.

He looked at her in surprise. "Why'd you do that?"

"Because you look like you just ate a green apple." Dara gave him a long-suffering glance. "This should make you feel better. Harrison told me that I should do what you say, and you'll take care of me."

Something shifted in his eyes and he became utterly still. "He really said that?"

She studied him for a moment, wondering at the spark of concealed longing in his eyes. "Yes, but it doesn't mean I'm gonna do it," she warned him. "I have an aversion to following orders from cretin bodyguard types."

"What about following suggestions from someone who cares about your safety? Someone who cares what happens to you," he returned.

"Be careful," Dara said, her heart swelling in her chest. "I might take that personally."

"Maybe you should."

She didn't breathe for a full minute. Never in her life had she wanted so much for a man to kiss her. Never had she wanted so much to kiss a man. To let her emotions spill over, to fill and be filled, to share the feeling and the wanting. She shook her head. Had she ever wanted something so much it hurt?

Never.

But Dara just wasn't strong enough to handle the risk of rejection right now. "You know, there's still a lot I wish I knew about you."

His eyes shuttered briefly, then he dipped his head. He looked as if he were tasting a particularly foul-tasting medicine. "Go ahead," he said reluctantly. "Ask."

She hid her grin and slipped out of his arms. Folding her hand inside his, she tugged him forward. "Favorite ice cream?"

"Homemade strawberry."

"When was the first time you had it?"

"My grandmother's backyard. She made it to celebrate my mother's homecoming."

Puzzled, Dara glanced up at him. "Homecoming?"

"She went to Hollywood for a while, wanted to be a star. It didn't work out, so she came back to Mississippi."

"Did you live with your mother after she moved back?"

Ridge threaded his fingers through hers. "Sometimes."

She sensed the darkness in him and wanted to push it back. "Name of the first girl you kissed," she said.

Ridge stopped and stared at her, his lips twitching. "Mary Beth Cannaday. I was thirteen."

Dara nodded. "Just out of curiosity," she continued, "how many women—?"

Ridge arched a dark eyebrow. "Are you sure you want to know?"

The tone of his voice, rough and sensual, sent a surge of awareness rippling along her nerve endings. "Maybe not," she conceded, and started walking again. "How many friends do you have?"

"A few," he said. "Not many. My life-style hasn't allowed it." There was a trace of regret, but mostly acceptance.

"Do you ever get lonely?"

He paused a beat. "Yeah."

"At night?"

He hesitated so long she thought he wasn't going to answer. "Yeah," he finally said, filling the one syllable with deep male need.

Dara sucked in a breath and looked away.

"What do you want from me, Dara?"

Her heart lodged in her throat. "Oh, no," she protested, pushing her hair behind her ear. "Don't ask that. Because I might just tell you. And you would do what you always do—pull back."

Frustration tightening his features, he wrapped his hands around her wrists, and suddenly she was captured. His hands were strong, yet careful of her. His eyes, fiery and potent, burned a path clear to her soul. "I want to be there for you, Dara, in every way you could think of." His voice deepened. "And probably a few ways you haven't thought of. There's a helluva lot I shouldn't do with you." He pulled her closer so that her legs rubbed against his strong thighs, and he slowly lowered his head. "Starting with this," he said in a rough whisper just before he took her mouth.

Her lips were still tingling four hours later. She stood under the shower, rinsing conditioner from her hair and wondering if she was really going to go through with it. She'd thought a shower might wash away Ridge's effects, but it hadn't. Her breasts were heavy, her nipples tight as if he'd caressed them for hours. But he hadn't. Her skin was sensitive, her nether region swollen with anticipation as if he'd fondled her so that she would be ready for him. But he hadn't.

He had kissed her mindless until she could barely stand, then set her away from him. Perhaps, if he'd left it at that, she *might* have eventually recovered. But he hadn't.

He'd watched her all evening.

Like a man craving every possible intimacy, he'd let his gaze play over her body. All through dinner she'd felt his heat, his need, his passion, until her skin grew so sensitized that clothing felt abrasive to her skin.

Dara turned the faucet off, stepped out of the shower, and buried her head in a towel. Her anxiety suddenly spiked, making it hard to breathe. Was she crazy? What if he turned her away?

Wrapping the towel around her head, she dismissed the notion. She couldn't think about that. Moving through her ritual of scented body lotion and light facial moisturizer, she added a spray of perfume and made her mind go blank. She might be scared spitless, but in her heart and soul, she knew it was time.

Ridge lay on his bed, his arms folded behind his neck, his eyes closed. He hadn't bothered to strip off his clothes or remove his gun holster. In his current frame of mind, he might as well have been in a barn instead of the comfortable guest room with the plush carpet and wide bed with the soft blue coverlet. Keeping his eyes closed, he suspected it didn't matter that he'd left the little brass bed-side lamp on low because he sure as hell wasn't sleepy.

He was excruciatingly aroused.

He'd never known a man could be so full from wanting a woman. So full his heart had trouble beating regularly, his lungs had difficulty allowing normal breathing, and his manhood was permanently begging for release.

If that weren't bad enough, Ridge was pretty sure his brain was swollen, too. That would explain why he could think of nothing but Dara.

He wrenched himself up to a sitting position and vented his frustration with a litany of self-directed oaths. In the middle of his tirade, Dara walked through his door.

He abruptly stopped, but she must have caught the tail end of it because her eyes widened to huge pools of blue. She stepped backward, nudging the door closed with a loud click that reverberated through the room.

She took a deep breath that made her chest rise and drew his attention to the floral satin robe that gently covered her curves all the way from her shoulders to her bare feet. His heart began to pound against his rib cage. Dara was dressed for bed, and she was less than three feet away from *his* bed.

Her hair hung damply to her shoulders, her scent, sensual and inviting, filled his pores when he breathed. She looked at him with a mixture of longing, determination, and uncertainty.

The uncertainty gave him half a shot at keeping his sanity in this situation. He cleared his throat.

As if she knew what he was going to say, she held up her hand. "Don't talk. Just listen."

He watched the smooth column of her throat tense in a nervous swallow just before she pushed away from the door. "I know you want me," she said quietly as she took slow steps toward him. "You say you have reasons why you can't be with me. Maybe you do. But I don't share your reasons. The only thing I share with you is the same overwhelming *need* to be together."

She dug her hand into the pocket of her robe and tossed several packets of condoms on the bed. Ridge stared at the packets and his heart seemed to stop. "Six. For God's sake—" He jerked his head toward her and speech left him.

She lowered her eyelids in a vulnerable yet seductive blink that blew his sensible refusal out of the water. His body started to hum and he searched for a safe place for his gaze, but everywhere he looked at her, he only got in deeper. The "I'm ready" expression she wore on her face made the air seem to crackle, and his blood pound. Her robe parted slightly as she placed one knee on his mattress and the bare, silky expanse of her thigh taunted him.

He clenched his hands into fists and told himself he would turn her away.

Putting her hand on his shoulder, she stretched forward, causing the robe to gap and reveal a tantalizing glimpse of her breasts. Ridge closed his eyes and felt her push the holster from his shoulder. He tried to find the will, tried to form the word *no*.

"I can't pretend anymore. I need you."

Her words scored his gut like lashes of a velvet whip. "Dara," he groaned.

"If you can't make love to me," she said, her voice twisting and seducing him with huskiness, "then let me make love to you."

She took her hand away, and he heard the whisper of her satin robe sliding from her body to the bed. The whisper was far more inviting than the harsh, condemning voice in his head. The tender touch of her lips brushing his cheek was more powerful than any regret he'd feel tomorrow.

She was everything he'd ever wanted, and couldn't have.

Taking a deep breath, he filled himself with her scent and opened his eyes. His heart squeezed at the sight of her.

Bare and beautiful, she sat before him all pale skin and womanly curves. Her pulse beat fast against her throat, and that tiny evidence of her excitement shredded his waning reserve.

Her shoulder bore a bruise, a badge of courage from the rally yesterday. Ridge's lips burned with the need to kiss the mark away. Her uptilted breasts, crowned with nipples like berries, rose and fell with each breath she took. Her waist curved into her hips that seemed designed for his hands. Lower still, between her creamy thighs, the downy fluff of hair hiding the secrets of her femininity made his body tighten further with the need to make her his. Ridge wanted her, but he wanted more than her body. He wanted her laughter, her passion, and her tenderness. God help him, he wanted her soul.

All his protests died in his throat. Reason was snuffed out. She was everything he'd ever wanted, and he could have her, if only for tonight.

Meeting her gaze, Ridge reached for her slim shoulders and pulled her to him. "Come here, beautiful. I'm dreaming with my eyes open tonight."

Her lips willingly met his. His heart swelled at her telltale sigh of relief. Her skin was cool, and he was certain he could warm her. With one delicate slide of her tongue against his, though, she incinerated his restraint. Before he knew it Ridge was lying across her on the bed. Elbows digging into the mattress so he wouldn't crush her, he wrapped his palms on either side of her jaw and tasted the sweet recesses of her mouth. So much to feel, so much to taste. Raw with need, he felt his muscles quake with the effort it took not to gorge himself on her.

Her soft little sounds vibrated in his mouth, and he tore his mouth away, rolling to her side. Lungs heaving, he shook his head. "Dara." Lifting an unsteady hand, he looked at her. "I'm afraid I'm gonna hurt you," he whispered hoarsely.

Her eyes locked with his, she shook her head and licked her swollen lips as if she liked the taste of him. Another knot tightened in his gut. Edging closer, she kissed his jaw and began to unbutton his shirt. "You won't."

She said it with such simplicity and confidence that he was knocked off kilter all over again.

"Would you think I'm terrible if I told you I've day-dreamed about how you'd look without your clothes?"

A rough chuckle squeezed past his dry throat. "No." He shrugged out of his shirt and started on the fastening of his jeans. "If that's all you've thought about, then—"

"It wasn't." Dara placed her hand on his stomach, making it ripple in response. Her gaze, baring her emotions, met his.

"I thought about a lot more," she said, and leaned closer to press her lips to his abdomen.

He sucked in a long breath. Her mouth, hovering just below his belly button, was entirely too close to the part of him that was filled with demanding need. She skimmed her lips slightly lower, then higher, up toward his chest, and Ridge didn't know whether to laugh or cry in relief.

In one quick movement he shucked his jeans and briefs, then pulled their lower bodies close together. Her mouth continuing its slow trek up his chest, she tangled her smooth, silky legs with his. She dipped her tongue around his nipple and he swore. "You're not making this easy for me."

She gave a breathless chuckle. "That's not my job."

Deliciously exasperated, he flipped her onto her back and stared at her. Her hair spread out on the coverlet like black satin. Her eyes were wide, her lips already swollen by his kisses.

"What are you doing?" she asked in a mildly accusing voice. As if she couldn't keep her hands off of him, she stretched her fingers through the hair across his chest. "I said I was going to make love to you."

His gaze flicked over her breasts. "There's no reason this can't be a joint effort, is there?"

Dara's eyes darkened. "No, but—"

"Good," Ridge said before he lowered his head to run his mouth over her breast.

Dara's breath hitched in her throat. "There's a lot I want to do," she warned him.

"We'll try to fit it all in." He drew deeply on her nipple and somewhere in that moment, while her heart raced beneath his mouth, he found a little of the control he'd almost lost.

His hands moved over every inch of her, his mouth praising everything from her neck to her toes. When he kissed the bruises on her cheek and shoulder to make them better, Dara fought tears.

"Hey, what's this?" he asked, frowning when his fingers caught the moisture from her eyes.

Dara bit her lip self-consciously. Maybe he didn't want her emotions handed to him on a platter. "You're being nice again."

"And it makes you cry. I don't want to do that." He skimmed his large callused hand over her rib cage and waist, down to the top of her thighs. His eyes darkened with sensual purpose. "Maybe I need to distract you."

His mouth swallowed anything she might have managed to say, and his fingers went on a seek-and-find journey to her most sensitive pleasure point.

Her restlessness tightening to an ache, Dara sucked Ridge's tongue deeper into her mouth. Ridge groaned and slipped his fingers inside her.

Her head began to swim, and she felt herself rapidly approaching the crest. She pulled her mouth away and stayed his hands. "No," she managed breathlessly. Her heart was beating so hard she had to blink to read the quizzical expression on his face. "I want you inside this time." She cupped her hand around his arousal and stroked. "All the way."

Ridge closed his eyes and swore. The muscles of his shoulders bunched beneath her touch. His hard chest, sprayed with crisp, tantalizing hair, crushed her breasts and teased her nipples. His powerful thighs planted firmly between hers. His rigid masculinity, heavy with promise, pressed against her.

Grabbing a condom, he tore open the packet and pulled it on. He pushed her thighs farther apart and, for a timeless moment, meshed his gaze with hers. His nostrils flared as he crouched, suspended over her body. She felt the heat and power rippling through him. What drew her most, however, was the ruthless possessiveness in his leonine eyes.

He lifted each of her hands to his broad shoulders. "Hold on," he told her in a rough voice.

Then, inch by excruciating inch, he took her, filling her so that she felt stretched beyond capacity. Dara held her breath and Ridge sucked in his. His face clenched as if he were in pain. "You are so incredibly tight."

A second passed, then two, then three. Her body began to accommodate his.

"Are you okay?" he muttered, his breath warm and ragged against her neck.

She moved against him, and he growled. She wriggled at the sensation of him inside her.

"Don't do that," he grated in a low voice.

Dara pressed herself against him and sighed at the sparks that shot through her bloodstream. "I... have this annoying... habit—" she moved again, and their moans mingled together "—of not always doing what you tell me to do. You feel good," she said huskily.

Ridge squeezed her bottom and eased himself slightly away. His hooded eyes filled with dark wonder, his jaw muscle ticking. "Every night," he told her in his velvet-

and-steel voice, "I've dreamed of being this close to you. Of being inside you." He pulled out of her and Dara immediately strained to get closer.

"Ridge," she pleaded with him when he gently held her on the bed.

He lowered his mouth to her nipple. "It'll be better," he promised, "if we take our time."

He moved and his arousal slid in an agonizingly erotic caress against, yet not inside her. The sensation nearly drove Dara arching off the bed. "I don't want to take our time! I've been waiting for—"

Dara gasped. He did it again, whatever it was, that rubbed his masculinity where she was swollen and achy. She wiggled restlessly against him. "*What* are you doing to me?"

His lips tilted into a predatory, possessive, almost grin. "You don't like it?"

"Yes. No." He moved again, and Dara felt her nerve endings jump in fits and starts. "Oh—" She bit her lip, fighting a trace of desperation. "Are you trying to torture me?"

His face shadowed with concern, and he gently kissed her neck. "No, I just want to make it good for you. Better than it's ever been."

Her heart tightened at his tenderness, but her body was clamoring, shamelessly demanding him. "You are," she managed. "But I need you closer." Loath to have any distance between them, Dara slid her legs around his hips and pulled him back in. "Now."

He stared deep into her eyes and twined one of his hands with hers. His other hand slid beneath her bottom, tilting her hips so that he penetrated more deeply.

"Is this close enough?"

Dara's mouth went dry. Unable to form a syllable, she gave a jerky nod.

Narrowing his eyes in sensual concentration, he started a slow, deliberate rhythm that had her womb tightening again. "Don't fight it. I want it all, Dara. Everything you've got."

Helplessly, Dara moved in counterpart, drinking in every sensation, the voluptuous slide of him against her, inside her, his breath on her face, their bodies slick with perspiration, titillating and stimulating with every movement against each other. With his eyes holding hers as he repeatedly sank deep inside her, Dara had never felt so intimately and completely claimed.

Pressure climbed inside her. She pressed her hand to his buttocks, urging him faster, harder, until everything seemed to narrow to desperate need.

Ridge must have seen. "Let go," he urged. He rubbed his thumb over the swollen pearl of sensation and she bowed into him, whispering his name. Again, he filled her, and again, he caressed her, until spasms burst through her. For one endless, timeless moment, she stiffened in his arms and melted into a river of ripples.

Just as she emerged from a haze of ecstasy, Ridge bucked, chanting her name. Thrusting inside her as far as he could go, he tightened his fingers around hers, his golden eyes glittering with pleasure, and soared over the edge.

It was as if a bomb had detonated in the room. The only sound for several moments was their labored breathing. He kissed her, then, with a groan, Ridge rolled over onto his back, keeping his hand laced with Dara's.

"You should have told me it's been a while for you. You were so tight I could have hurt you," he said, remembering how wide her eyes had gotten when he'd first slipped inside her. "Did I?"

"Hurt me?" Dara turned her head toward him and met his gaze. She didn't look hurt, he thought, thanking God. He'd felt like a wild man, yet she looked like a completely fulfilled woman. She bit her lip and her eyes widened in mock accusation. "Yes," she said, sighing dramatically. "I was in terrible pain when you made me wait." Then she ruined the performance with a sexy chuckle.

His heart tightened. She was joking to reassure him. Ridge shook his head and hauled her on top of him. "I was worried about you," he grumbled. "There *is* a discrepancy in size."

Dara nodded, her hair tickling his neck. "Yes, and I've read articles about how men don't like to be compared with each other. So I guess I shouldn't say that you've got the best body I've ever seen naked. And if I told you that you're such an incredible lover it's a wonder I didn't black out, would it make your—" she smiled a witchy smile "—head swell?"

Feeling that swell in all the right places, Ridge couldn't resist a grin. "Yeah. My head's swelling. So what are you gonna do about it?" He brought her mouth to his and kissed her the way he'd wanted to for weeks. The fact that he'd just had her didn't seem to matter. Slowly pulling back, he stared in wonder at her dazed expression. For the moment, this incredible, wonderful woman was his.

A part of him, deep inside, however, remained dark with doubt. *It won't last. He still had unfinished business with Montgomery. She won't want you when she finds out the truth.* The turbulence of his past rolled through him, but he pushed it away. He'd be damned if he let anything ruin these moments with Dara. He changed the subject back to her comment on comparisons. "It may be the twentieth century, Darlin' Dara, but sometimes a man still likes to pretend he's the only one."

Dara's eyes softened. "I don't think I'll have to pretend," she said solemnly. "I've forgotten every man but you."

Ridge felt another steel-reinforced concrete wall inside him shatter. The woman was more effective than a wrecking ball when it came to his defenses, yet she managed it with honesty and tenderness. He wondered what he'd ever done to deserve her, and knew he'd done nothing. Speechless, he pulled her closer and held her tight, wondering when pretending wouldn't work anymore, wondering when forgetting wouldn't be possible.

Eleven

The next morning Dara kept bumping into things. First her knee collided with her dresser, then she rammed her shin against the toilet. She finally woke up when she stubbed her toe on the bed frame.

Although she scolded herself in the mirror, she couldn't manage to wipe the glow off her face. Rolling her eyes at herself, she wondered if everyone would know that Dara Seabrook was in love with Ridge Jackson. It only took a second before she wondered if she cared if everyone knew.

After they'd made love again last night, Ridge had insisted she return to her room. She'd struggled with her disappointment until he'd confessed he didn't have a prayer of sleeping if she was in his room.

This morning, heaven help her, she was giddy. She dressed and coasted down the hall to his room, and this time she knocked.

Ridge opened the door and arched a dark eyebrow in inquiry.

Dara gave him a gentle shove backward, wrapped her arms around his neck, and kissed him. Dimly, she heard the click of the door closing before Ridge turned her little good-morning kiss into a full-blown reminder of last night.

When he finally pulled back, Dara just stared at him and swallowed hard. "G'morning," she managed in a shaky voice.

"Good morning," he growled. "Did you sleep well?"

Dara smiled. "Like a baby."

Ridge scowled and turned away. "I'm glad one of us did."

Concern washed over her. Her smile faded as she walked to his side. "But I thought that was the reason you wanted me to leave, because . . ."

"Yeah."

Watching Ridge run a hand through his hair, she noticed his hair was ruffled as if he'd plowed his hand through it several times. His clean-shaven jaw was marred by a couple of tiny scrapes and his eyes had shadows beneath them. On another person, those things might signal vulnerability. Ridge, however, looked rougher, more dangerous, and to Dara's despair, more remote than ever.

Her heart tightened, but she made herself remain calm. "You're not going to give me one of those morning-after-I-shouldn't-have-given-in-to-my-carnal-urges speeches, are you?"

Ridge sighed and met her gaze. "No. I couldn't regret last night, not one minute of it. But there are some things that last night can't change—that nothing can change."

"I wish you would tell me."

"No," he said firmly as soon as the words left her mouth.

vas hit with a tidal wave of exasperation and im-
"Then tell me you're not going to pretend that
make love." Breathing deeply, she took her

courage in hand. "Or that you're just my bodyguard. Or that I'm just another client."

"You were never just another client," he retorted, then paused, his golden eyes turbulent. "No. I'm not going to pretend, but I don't think you're going to be happy with the cards in this deck when they're all played out."

Dara frowned. Now what in the world did he mean by that? "Are you deliberately trying to confuse—"

"Dara," Rainy called from the end of the hallway. "Mr. Merriman wants you down here as soon as you can manage."

"You need to go," Ridge said, moving toward the door.

Torn by the apprehension she'd heard in Rainy's voice and the fact that everything was unsettled between her and Ridge, Dara stepped in front of him and put her hand on his arm. "I don't want to."

He stared at her hand for a long time, then covered it with one of his. "I know."

For the moment Dara put off responding to Rainy. "I need to know that you won't pull away from me." She heard the pleading note in her voice, but she couldn't hate herself for it. He'd become too important to her.

Ridge's face tightened. "You don't know what you're asking."

"Yes, I do. There is no one more important to me than—"

He covered her mouth and shook his head. "Don't say that. Not now."

Why? she wanted to yell. "Ridge," she said, and that one syllable seemed to convey all her longing.

Bowing his head as if he bore the weight of the world, he took a long breath and swore. "I can't promise you anything, but I can tell you there's never been anyone like you in my life." He lifted his head and seared her with his gaze. "Never." He removed her hand from his arm, then softened the action by kissing her fingers. He pushed open the door. "Let's see what Clarence wants."

The light of hope in Dara's eyes haunted Ridge as he followed her along the corridor, then down the stairs into the formal living room. With every step he was sure he'd lost his mind. He should have told her the truth, that anything between them stood a snowball's chance in hell. Instead, when he'd looked into her eyes he couldn't give her up.

He swore under his breath and glanced up to find Clarence in a major snit. The middle-aged man's complexion was mottled a purplish color and he was yelling into the phone. "What do you mean, we don't have a response for the press yet? We've got to counter this immediately!"

He crumpled a rag magazine in his hand and continued to fume a few more minutes, then hung up the phone. "It couldn't have happened at a worse time," Clarence said to Dara and Ridge. "Six days until the election, and look," he said, thrusting the paper at Dara, "at what we're facing."

"'New Breast Enlargement Pill Guarantees Four-Inch Results,'" Dara read in a puzzled voice.

Ridge resisted the urge to snicker.

Clarence shook his head. "Right-hand column."

"'Harrison Montgomery's Secret Son,'" she read in amazement. "'Mystery Cowboy the Result of Alien Union.'"

Ridge's blood drained to his feet. He gazed over Dara's shoulder and tried to read the article, but his eyes wouldn't focus. He felt as if he were in a spinning tunnel. In a distant, disconnected part of his mind, he heard Dara and Clarence.

"Has Drew called?"

"He says Harrison has never even met this guy."

"If they took the space creature out of the picture, I would have sworn it was a younger Harrison. Are you sure this isn't an old campaign picture?"

"The picture quality isn't very good, but that man isn't Harrison."

"What do we do now?"

"I'm waiting for a statement from Drew."

Dara swore and tossed the paper to the floor. "That slimy little weasel Willis Herkner wrote this nonsense. Can you imagine how much this will hurt Harrison and Helen? For years, they tried to have children. All those miscarriages..."

Clarence murmured something in agreement. But Ridge's attention snagged on the paper Dara had thrown away. Bending down, he carefully picked up the paper, straightened it, and began to read. Take out the alien part, change a few superficial facts, and this story could have been about him, Ridge realized with a sick feeling in his gut. According to the article, this poor guy lived out in the middle of nowhere in Wyoming. Ridge suspected the story was the result of the incumbent's panic over Montgomery's strong lead in the polls.

But then he took a good, hard look at the picture.

A chill ran down his spine. This man had the same bone structure, the same posture, and he'd bet the same eyes as Harrison Montgomery.

Could it possibly be true?

Ridge narrowed his eyes. If the old man had played around and fathered one baby, why couldn't he have done it twice? A dry chuckle wheezed from Ridge's throat. What incredible irony. If it were true.

Dara's voice broke through his gaze. "Ridge, why are you laughing? This is serious."

Carefully folding the article, Ridge shrugged. "I guess the alien angle got to me." He cleared his throat and backed away, needing space, lots of it. "This is one of those PR things—not my area. I'm going for a run."

She tilted her head to one side thoughtfully. "You look a little strange," she said quietly. "Are you okay?"

As okay as you can be when you've just learned you're not the only living bastard of the future president of the United States of America. He wasn't going to lie. "I could use some air."

He felt Dara's gaze as he jogged up the stairs, but Ridge just kept right on going. How could he articulate to Dara what he couldn't explain to himself?

He spent the day running. Technically, he hit the road three times, but the rest of the time he avoided human contact. It wasn't that difficult, since Dara and Clarence were on conference calls with campaign headquarters most of the day. Ridge skipped regular mealtimes and grabbed sandwiches for lunch and dinner.

By midnight he should have been dead on his feet, but his mind was still spinning. After checking on Dara as she slept, he went down to the exercise room and started his weight-lifting routine.

That was where Dara found him thirty minutes later.

She entered the room and immediately felt his tension. The air seemed to seethe and burn with restlessness. It matched her own churning emotions. After the briefings, she'd been mentally exhausted, yet physically keyed up. The couple of hours of rest had only served to tease her body, and her fury at Willis Herkner soared through her like a boomerang. She took a deep, relaxing breath. It didn't work. "I haven't seen you all day," she said, leaning against the cool basement wall.

Ridge looked up and wiped his forehead with the back of his hand. "You've been busy."

"Not that busy."

He didn't say anything, instead continued the chest press repetitions.

Dara envied him the ability to focus his energy and control it. "Have you been avoiding me?"

"You and everybody else."

"Including yourself."

He stopped and wiped his face with a towel. "Maybe." Swinging his leg over the bench, he walked toward her and studied her. With his prowling gait and rippling muscles, he reminded her again of a lion. "I checked on you a little while ago. Why aren't you asleep?"

Dara stared at him and felt the threat of distant thunder roll through her bloodstream. He wore no shirt and his body glistened with a faint sheen of perspiration. Clean, honest sweat from a strong, hungry man. The hunger glowed in his eyes.

She felt the heat of it and that distant thunder rolled a little closer. His chest and arm muscles were pumped from his workout, and the running shorts he wore did little to hide his powerful thighs and the bulge of his masculinity. She knew, intimately, the strength of his body. She knew, intimately, the power of his desire.

She was attracted at her most basic and primitive level. Edgy need rippled through her. "I couldn't sleep."

He cupped her jaw, his gaze saying *Little girl go home.* "Maybe you should count sheep."

In no frame of mind to be patronized, she jerked her head away. "I'm angry. Furious that a slimy little weasel like Willis Herkner can slander and get away with it. I've got too much energy to just lay down and count sheep."

Ridge narrowed his eyes, then shook his head. "I'm not in the mood for talking about some weasel reporter tonight."

"Then what are you in the mood to talk about?"

His gaze locked with hers. "I'm not in the mood for talking, Dara," he said, his voice softer than velvet.

She knew the answer before she asked, knew the outcome before he opened his mouth, but she asked it anyway. "What are you in the mood for?"

His nostrils flared. "Go to bed. I don't have a gentle, patient bone in my body right now."

Her blood kicking through her, she stood her ground. "You didn't answer my question."

His jaw muscle ticked. "From you?" he clarified.

Dara nodded.

"I don't want questions. I don't want candles. I don't want romance." He paused half a beat. "I want sex."

Dara held her breath. She'd known what was coming, but the bold, blunt statement still managed to resound through her like a shock wave.

Taking in her shocked expression, he lowered his eyelids in grim satisfaction. "There. Are you happy? Women want romance and tenderness and lots of time. I don't—"

Dara found her voice. "I'm not most women."

His whole body seemed to tighten. "You don't know what you're getting into."

Maybe she didn't know. With a knowledge deeper than desire, however, she knew she wanted to be with him whenever and however she could. He was angry and needy, she could feel it. She was angry and needy, too. "I want to find out."

Fire sparked in his eyes, and he ran his gaze over her robe. When she'd gone searching for him, she'd wondered if he would attach the same significance to the garment that she did. She felt her breasts swell beneath her nightshirt, beneath her robe.

He wrapped his hand around her waist and tugged her closer, then slipped his other hand into her pocket, skimming her thigh through the satin material. His touch sent a shocking spasm of sensation to her core. He pulled a condom from the pocket. "What a good girl," he muttered against her mouth, sucking her lower lip. "You came prepared."

Then he pushed off her robe, wrapped his hard, warm hands around her bottom, and took her mouth. He rotated her pelvis against his in blatantly erotic movements designed to stimulate her and himself.

Dara was instantly hot, immediately out of control. Ridge pulled her nightshirt over her head and lifted her so that he could take her breast into his mouth. She wrapped her legs around his waist and squirmed against his probing masculinity. He pumped against her. If she'd been rid of her silky panties and he'd ditched his shorts, he'd be inside her.

The thought drove her mad.

He lowered her feet to the floor and brushed his hand over her panties. His eyes glittered with arousal. "You're wet," he said, and discarded the peach triangle of fabric.

He kissed her hard in approval, then dropped to his knees and held her hips firmly in his hands. "You're so sweet, so sexy. I want you like this."

Dara tensed. "I—"

His mouth caressed her intimately. She closed her eyes against the ruthlessly sensual invasion of his tongue. His voracious lips rendered her mindless and mute. She could barely breathe. With devastating ease, he pushed her past the limit and over. Then he did it again.

The second time her knees buckled beneath her. She whimpered her release, and he caught her, shifting her to the mat. With a conqueror's eyes, he watched her as he shoved down his shorts and rolled on the condom.

In some corner of her mind she thought she'd like to help him do that sometime. Right now she was doing well to lift her heavy arms to his shoulders as he slowly slipped inside her.

They both sighed.

"You feel so good," he said in a rough voice as he stretched in a wonderfully agonizing rhythm. "I don't know if I'll ever get enough of you."

She arched into him and gave a breathless moan. "I hope not." She flexed her inner muscles and watched him suck in a deep breath.

"What did you do?" he growled.

Feeling incredibly voluptuous, she repeated it, reveling in his response. "Like it?"

"*Like it?*" Staring at her, he swore. "Where the hell did you learn to do that?" he whispered.

Dara felt a euphoric rush and laughed. Her release had taken the edge off her tension. "In a magazine. This is the first time I've tried it." She bit her lip, feeling the impending buzz of another climax. "I can stop it if you don't like it."

"Stop?" He groaned.

She flexed again and watched him close his eyes in pleasure. He kissed her and the spicy flavor of their lovemaking made her heady. She battled against her own completion. This time she wanted to be there for all of his. Fluidly, he pumped. She squeezed. The combination set off an incredible chain of sensations.

Ridge dropped his mouth to her neck and suckled. A second passed and his body jerked into hers. For a long intense moment he shuddered, as gloriously out of control as she.

"Your turn," he muttered tenderly against her throat, and skimmed his hand down between them. Once, twice, three times, he touched her, and her body exploded.

Moments later he pulled on his clothes and helped her into her robe. He carried her up the stairs and tried to lay her on the bed, but Dara held on to his hand. She wanted him with her, but was hesitant to ask. The times he'd refused her had left their mark.

His gaze softened. "I'll stay."

"You knew without me asking," she said, struck by a powerful sense of wonder.

He shifted his fingers through her hair. "You don't hide much from me."

"You don't sound totally happy about it."

He sighed. "I'm not used to it. I'm not used to seeing what I see in your eyes."

As if the words couldn't hold themselves back, she burst, "Then you know I love you."

Ridge went completely still. "You don't know everything about me."

"I don't have to," she said. The doubt in his eyes made her want to weep. Dara sat up. "What can I do to prove it to you?" She searched his gaze. "Tell Harrison? Tell the world? Send out a press release?"

Ridge shook his head emphatically, but Dara kept on.

"Should I fire you so you don't have to protect me? So that we don't have this bodyguard/client relationship in the way? What do you want from me?" Frustration welled inside her and her deepest emotions spilled from her lips. "I'll give you my body, my heart. I'll give you a baby. What—"

He pressed his hand over her mouth. "Stop." He swallowed audibly and shook his head again. "You don't need to prove anything to me. And firing me wouldn't make a damn bit of difference. I'm taking care of you whether I'm on the payroll or not." He slipped his hands to her shoulders, his voice forceful, but his touch gentle. "Do you really think I could trust another man to protect you?"

Dara could feel the power of her feelings for Ridge vibrating back to her with the same intensity, if not more. She took a breath and felt the slightest easing inside herself. Although the future was uncertain, Ridge obviously cared for her. She placed her hand over his heart. "I just need you to know that I love you."

Ridge's chest expanded in a deep breath beneath her palm. His heart thundered in a pounding rhythm as he covered her hand with his. Staring at her with wonder, as if she were some sort of magic apparition that could disappear any moment, he whispered, "I know."

The next morning, Ridge woke to the sensation of a ticking clock inside him. A regular, persistently monotonous rhythm reminded him of passing seconds, minutes, hours, and days. Keeping a tight rein on Dara's exposure later that day as she went from radio interview to newspaper interview to television talk show in a last-dash media blitz, he was ever conscious of time going by.

Five days until the election.

Five days until he would be forced to leave Dara for good.

And what had he accomplished? The question haunted him as he watched Dara answer questions on a radio talk show. He still burned with hate for Harrison Montgomery. Somewhere along the way, however, he'd gotten sidetracked from his quest for revenge. Somehow along the way, his fascination with Dara had managed to overshadow the loss that drove him.

His lips quirked as he watched her share a moment of chagrin with the disc jockey when a commercial announcement didn't play on time. Who would have thought that underneath the PR polish, Dara Seabrook would connect with him, an unpolished bastard, on every possible level, some levels Ridge hadn't even known existed?

Who would have thought she could look at him as if he were the only man in the world? Ridge's gut tightened at the memory of her words. *I'll give you a baby.* She'd nearly given him a heart attack.

For just a moment, after they'd made love again and she had fallen asleep, Ridge had watched her and indulged in the seductive, dangerous fantasy of having Dara in his life permanently. It was difficult for him to imagine, because there'd been no single constant human presence in his life—not his grandmother, not his mother, and certainly not his father. The image became clearer, though, and it hit him with such a painfully sweet beauty that he'd shut his mind to it. The gap between possibility and reality made him want to ram his fist through the wall. He hated that he couldn't have her. More, though, he hated that he would have to hurt her.

On the second day of the publicity blitz, Ridge fought against a chafing restlessness that escalated every time he heard Dara defend Harrison and refute the possibility that her godfather had fathered an illegitimate child. After two radio shows and a newspaper interview, he was sure he would lose his lunch if he heard her defense one more time. Her appearance on a live afternoon talk show, however, guaranteed more of the same.

"One last caller," the hostess said. "Will, you're on the air with Dara Seabrook."

"Miss Seabrook," a man's whiny voice came over the airwaves, "how can you be sure your godfather didn't get a woman pregnant and dump her and the kid? He could have done it before you were even born."

Dara stiffened in shock at the insulting words the man chose. Precious seconds of dead silence passed before her brain made the connection. *Will was Willis Herkner.* Fury roared in her ears. What she wanted to say would have to be censored. She took a deep, calming breath. "It's difficult for some people to understand the concept of character. While it's true that I couldn't possibly have known Harrison Montgomery before I was born, I know what his character is. Harrison saved my father's life. He's not the kind of man who could turn his back on his own child."

"A touching side issue. Why don't you grant an interview with the *American Investigator* so you can tell your side of the story?"

Dara bared her teeth in what she hoped resembled a smile. "Oh, I don't think they would be interested in hearing from me, Will. You see, I have this habit of telling the truth." Drew would either kiss her or kill her for what she was about to say, Dara was sure. "Most people know the *Investigator* isn't a serious news publication. Their forte is rumor, grossly inaccurate gossip, and unfounded speculation. Tabloids are great for killing time in a checkout line at the grocery store or for lining bird cages, but that's about it."

"Why you bi—"

The producer disconnected Willis's line and the hostess cleared her throat. "We're about out of time. Thanks so much to our guest, Dara Seabrook," she said, and made her closing comments.

Within moments Dara was safely settled in the back of her limo with Ridge. The cellular phone was already ringing. She groaned and buried her head in his shoulder. "Do I have to take that call?"

"Want me to?"

"Please," she murmured as she stretched her arms around his back. Breathing his scent in deeply, she felt a strong sense of satisfaction despite her weariness. Here was where she wanted to be.

"Jackson," Ridge said, toying with her hair.

Dara felt him tense, then deliberately relax as he stretched his legs and let out a measured sigh. "She's beat, Drew. She'll call you back."

Dara heard the buzzy murmur of Drew's reply, but was unable to distinguish his words.

Ridge muffled a chuckle. "Yeah, she made that comment about bird cages even though it wasn't in the script you gave her."

More buzzy murmurs followed.

"Before you get too upset, you should know she almost told that last caller what he could do with his magazine before he took a trip straight to hell."

Dead silence.

Dara peeked up at Ridge. He rolled his eyes. "Call Dara tomorrow. 'Bye," he said to Drew, then urged Dara's lips closer to his. "You know, I almost like that guy when he closes his mouth." Ridge grinned. "Funny. I like your mouth open or shut." And he proceeded to demonstrate how much he liked her mouth until her lips went numb.

A seed of hope grew inside Dara. If Ridge could joke, and talk, and make love with her, maybe they could make it work. Maybe he wouldn't leave after election day. Although she never forgot his insistence that they couldn't be together, she pushed back the shadow of her doubts and steeped herself in his attention.

After a dinner filled with easy conversation and warm, meaningful glances, she took a shower while he waited in her room.

Toweling her hair dry, she stepped through the open connecting doorway and saw him seated in a desk chair, studying the copy of the *American Investigator*. Dara frowned. She'd thought she'd thrown it away. Walking closer, she touched his shoulder. "Where did you find that?"

Startled, Ridge quickly folded the paper and tossed it on her desk. "In the trash where it belongs." He stood up from his chair and shoved his hands into his pockets.

Puzzled by his manner, she gazed at him thoughtfully. "I thought you weren't interested in campaign business."

His gaze cooled. "I'm not."

"Then why—"

Ridge shrugged. "I wondered who the guy in the picture was."

Dara unfolded the tabloid on the desk. "He does look exactly like Harrison."

"Do you know who he is?"

Dara shook her head, wondering again at his odd tone. "You haven't had much to say about this."

"What's to say?" he replied with forced nonchalance. "It's either the truth or it isn't."

Apprehension raced through her. "Well, you don't actually believe the story, do you?"

Ridge shrugged again. "It doesn't matter what I believe. I don't talk to reporters."

Dara gaped at him. "You can't honestly believe this stupid tabloid story about an alien mating with my godfather."

Ridge narrowed his eyes. "I don't buy the alien part, but the man in that picture looks a helluva lot like Montgomery." He glanced down at the paper as if compelled by something deep inside him.

Dara felt confused and alarmed. Her intuition told her something wasn't right, something important wasn't right. "You haven't been a fan of Harrison's from the beginning. Now that I think of it, your dislike of him has seemed almost personal." Suddenly afraid, she crossed her arms over her chest. "What's going on?" she demanded. "When did you know him before?"

His gaze meshed with hers and he went very still. The cold expression in his eyes fueled her fear. "I'd never met Harrison Montgomery before the MTV taping," he said in a lethal, quiet voice.

Dara trembled, but she felt as if she'd picked the lock on Pandora's box and was compelled to open it. "Then why are you so interested in that story?" she asked. "You're always ready to point out something negative about him. You must have had some experience with him, even if it was indirectly. Something."

Ridge turned away, saying nothing.

Dara's heart twisted. Stepping forward so she could see his set face, she could feel Armageddon coming. "You hate him," she concluded.

Ridge glared at her. "I told you, I don't like politics."

"You hate him."

"Don't push me on this, Dara," he warned.

Chilled to the bone, Dara began to shake from the inside out. Heaven help her, though, she needed answers. She took a careful, shallow breath. "You hate him."

The blood drained from his face and something inside him seemed to snap. "Yes-s," he hissed from between gritted teeth. "I hate him."

The power of his antipathy stunned her. She immediately pulled back. Her mind went blank. She opened her mouth and tried to make her lips form the word why, but no sound came out.

Ridge stepped closer, his expression tight with bitterness, his chest expanding from his deep breaths. "I've got a damn good reason to hate Harrison Montgomery since you're so curious. Maybe it's time I finally told you why." He pointed his index finger to his chest. "That sonofabitch is my father."

Dara shook her head. It was impossible. It couldn't be true. It couldn't . . . "How?" she managed feebly. "There must be a mistake. He couldn't have—"

"There was a mistake," he said in a deadly firm voice. "And I'm it." When she didn't respond, he gave a dry, humorless chuckle. "You don't believe me, do you? All this time I didn't want to tell you because I knew the truth would hurt you like hell."

Dara couldn't put a sentence together. The evening had turned surreal. She could hear Ridge. She could see him. But she couldn't feel a thing.

"You're thinking that I don't look like him. You're right. I don't. Except for one feature." He lowered his head closer to hers. "Look at my eyes."

Dara stared into his lion eyes, golden eyes the same color as her godfather's. And the room began to spin.

Twelve

It took several moments for Dara to catch her breath. Racing in different directions at Mach speed, her mind, however, was a totally different matter. She covered her eyes and shook her head. *Think,* she told herself, then looked up at Ridge. "How? When?" She lifted her hands helplessly.

"How is obvious," he said dryly. "My mother went to Hollywood, had a few bit parts in some B-grade movies, and took in everything Tinseltown had to offer. That included wild parties and a six-week affair with Harrison Montgomery."

Confused, Dara wrinkled her brow. "But I thought you said she went to Hollywood *after* you were born."

"That was the second time."

Dara chewed the inside of her lip. "It doesn't make sense. Harrison wouldn't have gotten involved with your mother. He was already—" Realization hit her and she stopped abruptly, her stomach plunging. "Married," she finished in a whisper.

"Yeah," Ridge said, his voice full of bitter irony. "Married."

"Your mother. Did she tell Harrison? Did he know?"

"She tried. She left messages at his office, but they had already broken off the affair. She came home to Mississippi for the rest of the pregnancy, then went back to Hollywood as soon as she could."

Dara shook her head again. Her world felt as if it had been turned upside down. "This is all so unreal. I don't know what to make of it. When did she tell you about Harrison?"

Ridge's gaze went shuttered. "The night she died of an overdose. I was sixteen."

Horrified, she felt a lump grow in her throat. "Oh, God," she whispered, reaching for him.

Ridge stepped back, and Dara felt her heart splinter. "It was a long time ago," he said.

But Dara could see that it might as well have been yesterday. Ridge had suffered for years, and someone needed to make it better. Someone needed to make it right. "We've got to tell Harrison."

"No." There wasn't an ounce of give in his voice.

Dara stared at him. "But—"

His fists were clenched, his face taut with anger, and his eyes were colder than ice. "I've gone my whole life without him. I don't need him now."

For an instant, regret shimmered in his face, then his expression became so remote it frightened her. "Now you know why we can't be together." He gave a curt shake of his head when she would have broken in. "I hate Harrison Montgomery as much as you love him."

Dara reeled at his statement as if she'd been knocked to the floor. She blinked to clear her head, to try to make some sense of the incredible situation, but her mind and heart twisted and turned. And before she could begin to take it in, Ridge was gone. Her heart squeezed painfully. She wanted to cry out, to go after him.

But she didn't know what to say.

Ridge tore off his clothes and pulled on his running shorts. He *needed* to run as fast and as far as his legs would carry him. He crammed his feet into running shoes and nearly tripped over Rainy as she came up the stairs.

"Excuse me," he muttered, and was out the front door. The night was pitch black. It suited his mood. He wanted to hide from reality, from Dara, from his thoughts, and from his heart.

As he pounded the pavement, thoughts of his mother, Harrison, and Dara swirled in his head. He wondered if the guy in the tabloid picture was another one of Harrison's *mistakes*. If so, Ridge had a half brother. He didn't know how to feel about that, didn't know how to feel about anything anymore. The only thing he was sure of was the incredible sense of loss over never holding Dara again.

The knowledge tore at him, no matter how fast or how far he ran. He struggled with the image of the lost expression on her face. Part of him wished he hadn't told her. Part of him was relieved that he had. The ugly secret was out, and as he'd suspected, she wouldn't be able to handle it.

Hours later, Ridge stood under the shower and began the slow, deliberate process of shutting his mind and heart against Dara Seabrook. It was a matter of survival. With the hot water beating against his skin, he recounted the tactics for keeping his mind focused on his job. He would keep it strictly business. He would avoid personal conversation, he told himself. He would forget that he'd made love to her. He would forget the sound of her laughter. He would forget her scent.

Inhaling a deep breath that seemed to carry her unique, sultry scent, he groaned and swore. It would be easier to forget his name.

When the shower curtain was pushed back, he jerked around to find Dara stepping into the tub with him. Her eyes glistened with shed tears, her face was solemn, yet determined, and she was completely naked.

Ridge's heart shot to his throat. He turned back around to stare at the tile. Every muscle in his body tensed. "Go away," he muttered.

"No," she said, softly, firmly.

He swore under his breath. "You don't belong here."

"Yes, I do."

She put her hands on his back, and he felt the heat of her close to his body. Ridge closed his eyes. "It'll never work. I'm leaving the day after the election," he warned her, his voice sounding rough to his own ears.

Her hands slid around his waist and her breasts nuzzled his back. "Then you'll go knowing that I love you more than anything."

His lungs crowded his chest. The trembling note in her voice undid him. Ridge glanced up at the ceiling and whispered, "Dara."

He felt her lips against his skin and heard a sweet broken sob. "I'm not leaving," she told him. "Not now."

Unable to bear the sound of her pain, he turned and gathered her into his arms. "Why are you doing this?"

"I already told you," she said, pressing her mouth against his chest. "I love you."

Frustration and arousal pumped through his body. "But—"

Distress written on her face, Dara shook her head. "Ridge, you're hurting, and I can't stand to be apart from you. I just can't."

Ridge's heart was so full he wondered if it would burst. He lowered his mouth to her forehead and sipped a drop of water from her skin. Dara closed her eyes and buried her face in his chest.

There were no words for what her presence did for him. He had been alone, always. Now he wasn't. That she hurt for him filled him with wonder.

She looked up and he saw the purest love shining in her eyes. For him. He had expected rejection. She offered acceptance.

She slipped her hands behind his neck and gently urged his lips to hers. Her tongue slipped inside his mouth, bringing a sigh of sweet longing from him. She kissed him again until the familiar thud of arousal beat out his earlier confusion.

Slowly pulling away, Dara looked up at him with dark eyes. "Let me make you feel better tonight," she whispered.

"You already have," he confessed, running his hands along the satin-slick skin of her waist and hips.

A ghost of a feminine smile tilted her lips just before she pressed her mouth to his throat. "I'm not finished."

Passion and trust, an irresistible combination, swelled inside him. She had become more than a craving, more than a physical need. He put himself in her hands, and the response she drew from him was so swift and powerful he shook with it.

She caressed his chest with kisses that alternately soothed and aroused. Her hands skimmed down his arms to the tips of his fingers and lifted his hands to her breasts. Cupping the swollen mounds, he toyed with her nipples and caught her moan with a deep kiss.

Dara shuddered and pulled back as if she were struggling for a sense of control. She shook her head. "You're making me forget all my plans."

The water temperature was still hot, but Ridge was hotter. He nudged his aching arousal against her warm belly and dipped his head to kiss her shoulder. "We could improvise."

"No," she murmured softly, then brushed her hand down his hip and across his abdomen to his arousal.

Ridge sucked in a quick, short breath.

Holding his gaze, she caressed his rigid length lightly, then returned her hand to his hip.

He withheld a tortured groan. He wanted to lift her onto his shaft and pump. Battling for control, Ridge closed his eyes. "I think," he said in a rough voice, "you better tell me about these plans."

Dara gave a husky laugh and slipped her tongue out to taunt one of his nipples. "You'll see," she assured him.

Ridge would have argued, but her hand skimmed over him again. He couldn't have formed a word if he'd tried. The sensation of her breasts against his ribs and her silky legs rubbing against his added to his insanity.

A moment didn't pass before her lips moved over his belly and the tips of her breasts tantalized the skin of his pelvis. Ridge's abdomen tightened.

Her mouth glanced his inner thigh and he opened his eyes. "Dara—" he began, not knowing what to say when he saw her head inches from his arousal.

She glanced up, and with her eyes completely focused on his, she kissed him there where he was hard and aching.

The sensation of her mouth made him wild. A rough growl vibrated from his throat. Control slipped from his grasp. He tried to pull back.

Dara shook her head. "Let me," she said, and closed her mouth over him.

A soft litany of oaths echoed off the tile walls until Ridge's voice broke. Her wet mouth and tongue seduced him past sanity. A haze of passion muddled his vision. As if through a fog, he watched her tenderly attend to him. Erotic as the act was, Ridge found his heart was just as affected as his body.

Let me make you feel better, she'd said with a desperate need to show him glowing in her eyes. With her mouth, with her body, Dara wanted to comfort. Everything about her spoke love to him. She only wanted to love. Him.

His own deep need broke through, surging through him, racing. All barriers burst to smithereens. All the reasons why he couldn't be with her dissolved. She had changed him. Whether he liked the fact or not was incidental. She was his, and he was hers.

His body shuddered, a direct consequence of her caresses and his realization that she was vital to his life. Craving the ultimate closeness with Dara, he slid his fingers through her wet hair and urged her head up to his. ''I need you.''

A single tear streamed down her cheek. ''Oh, Ridge.''

He lifted her against the tiled wall and slipped inside her. She wrapped her legs around his waist and clung for all she was worth.

His heart trembled. ''Home,'' he muttered, and his release surged through him.

The next morning Dara persuaded Clarence to make a substitute appearance for her while she tried to get in touch with Harrison. She'd spoken to him just before the tabloid story hit, and Dara wanted some answers of her own now. She had happily done her best to promote Harrison for the past year of her life, and she still believed he would be the president the country needed. She wouldn't, however, lie to cover his past sins. Neither would she jeopardize her relationship with Ridge.

By evening Harrison still hadn't returned her calls, and Dara reached another decision. She was going to find out who the man in the tabloid picture was, with or without Harrison's blessing.

While Dara and Ridge sat on the couch in the den and listened to a jazz CD, she tentatively broached the subject that had been bothering her all day. "Do you think you'll ever tell Harrison that you're his son?"

His gaze instantly wary, Ridge stiffened and set down his after-dinner coffee. "Not anytime soon."

She drummed her fingers on the top of the sofa. "I just wish there was a way—"

"There isn't," he interrupted. "This isn't one of those fairy tales where the father greets the long-lost son with open arms."

Troubled, Dara frowned. "We don't know how he'll react, since he may not even know he has a son."

"I don't give a damn how he would react." Ridge stood and made his way over to the fireplace.

Dara heard the male pride blaring out past years of disappointment. Sighing, she rose and followed him. "Maybe you hate him, but it bothers you. It pokes at you. I don't know what you went through, but from the outside looking in, it looks like unfinished business."

When he kept that don't-give-a-damn expression on his face, she went on, waving her hand as she tried to explain. "It's like a song without the end note. It's never resolved, and you're always left wondering 'what if.'"

"I don't want to make friends with him," Ridge said flatly. "I'd just as soon see him burn in hell."

Dara's heart twisted. She set her hand on his arm and felt the tension emanating throughout him. "I don't believe you hate him that much."

His eyes flared with anger. "Then you're wrong. I've spent the better part of my life wanting revenge against him."

So much hate, she thought, trembling under the force of it. She worried that such bitterness could destroy Ridge. She worried that it might consume him. The only truth that comforted her was that in this instance Ridge's words were far louder than his actions. "If you'd really wanted to, you've had all kinds of opportunities to get revenge on Harrison. Why haven't you done it?''

He glanced at her thoughtfully, then looked away. "You know why."

Nonplussed, she laced her fingers through his. "No, I really don't."

He tugged her closer and met her gaze. "Then you underestimate your power. The reason I haven't nailed Montgomery to the wall is because of you."

Dara pondered Ridge's words the next day as she rode to meet Harrison for a luncheon in Washington, D.C. It was the day before the election and for the first time in years she was uncomfortable about seeing her godfather. Ridge had little to say, but the warning glint in his eyes made it clear that he didn't want her disclosing his secret to Harrison.

Sighing, Dara picked up the sports section and stared at it unseeingly in the limousine. A few minutes later she flicked on the CD player.

Ridge's hand covered hers. "You're restless," he said.

"And you're quiet," she returned, and smiled because she couldn't hide anything from Ridge. "What's the matter? Did I wear out the super-bodyguard?"

A sexy grin played around his mouth, and he shook his head. "You wore out the man, not the bodyguard." He laced his fingers through hers. "What's bothering you?"

Dara glanced out the window at the windy fall day. "I haven't seen or talked to Harrison in a while. I feel strange about seeing him today, wondering what I'll say."

"Because of me."

"Partly," she admitted. "But I have other questions I'd like answered." Like why Harrison hadn't returned her calls. She shrugged. "Part of it is just the end of the campaign. The pace has been so frantic." Dara didn't want to dwell on the things that pulled Ridge apart from her. She turned back to him. "I need some help deciding which sunny island I should visit after tomorrow. Do you have any suggestions?"

Ridge searched her face. Her sudden change of subject took him by surprise. The image of Dara clad in a nothing-bikini lying on the sand or on the deck of a boat made his blood temperature rise. He wondered if she intended to go alone. "There's the Caribbean if you want to get there fast. Bermuda would be a little chilly. Tahiti's a long flight, but it's worth it."

She cocked her head to one side consideringly. "Which would you pick?"

His eyebrows rose. "I'm not going."

Her eyes widened. "Oh, you're not?" She made a tsking sound. "That could make things challenging for me."

"What do you mean?"

She leaned closer. "I've decided I want to make up for drowning myself in the campaign this past year, so I'm going to do some of the things I've never done before. Snorkel, and scuba dive, and—" she stretched her lips in a secret smile "—make love on the beach. If you're not coming with me, I'll have to cross making love on the beach off my list." She sighed and pursed her lips in a moue of concern. "Unless, I…well, do you think I could find someone else who—"

"You witch." His heart pounded against his rib cage as he tugged her onto his lap. He still had a tough time believing she was real and that she was really his. "If you're making love on the beach, then you're doing it with me."

Dara's smile returned. "Then I can keep it on the list?" She curled her hands around his neck and slid her fingers up the back of his neck.

Ridge growled. "I should be able to accommodate you." He lowered his mouth to hers for a long, voluptuous kiss that he reluctantly ended when the limo pulled to a stop outside the plush D.C. hotel.

Her eyes glazed with passion, she shook her head. "You don't play fair. How am I supposed to make intelligent conversation with Capitol Hill bigwigs after that kiss?"

She was so charmingly honest, Ridge wondered if there was anything he wouldn't do for her. Lifting her off his lap, he reluctantly set her away from him. "My heart's breaking for you, especially after that crack about making love on the beach."

He got out of the limo and looked in both directions. No press or protestors in sight, he noted with approval. Offering his hand, he glanced at her carefully and saw the nerves returning as she bit her lower lip. Ridge wanted to kiss her anxiety away. "You okay?"

She squared her shoulders and stood. "I'm fine," she insisted, walking into the hotel. He could practically hear her public persona clicking into place. By the time they reached the luncheon, he would have sworn she'd forgotten him if she hadn't squeezed his hand and whispered, "I love you. I want you to remember that."

Ridge's throat tightened. "I will," he murmured.

She waved at Drew and a congressman beckoning her from across the room. "I also want you to think about the fact that I've never made love in a limo." She turned her gaze directly to his with the force of a woman who knew what she wanted, and what she wanted was him. "Think you can accommodate me?"

Before he could tell the stinker he would *accommodate* her *anytime, anyplace,* she sashayed her way to the head table.

As the luncheon proceeded, Ridge watched with a detached eye. Several men made speeches pronouncing Montgomery the winner by a landslide. With less enthusiasm, Ridge concurred with their pronouncement. Montgomery would win, and Ridge conceded that the politician might actually make a decent president. If such an anomaly existed.

He wondered how he could have such mixed feelings about another human being. Usually, his character assessments were rapid and definitive; good, bad, or neutral. He tried to picture Montgomery thirty years ago. What kind of man had he been? In the years since then, was it possible that he had changed?

The prospect unsettled Ridge and made him question his hate. He might have pondered it longer, but one of the Secret Service men tipped him off that a large crowd had formed outside the hotel. A loud demonstration had begun.

When the luncheon was over, Ridge and Dara followed Harrison Montgomery, his wife Helen, and the Secret Service agents out of the hotel. Ridge tensed when he saw the same extremist group that had been responsible for the trouble at Dara's rallies.

"I want you in the car as soon as possible," he muttered to Dara.

Ever the politician, Montgomery waved to the crowd. A reporter asked what he thought of the demonstration, and Montgomery just smiled. "This is one of the great things about our country. Everyone has the right to free speech."

Ridge pulled Dara toward the limo.

Obviously determined to play this one to the hilt instead of sticking to the original plan, Montgomery urged Helen toward their car and stepped toward Dara's limo.

Ridge swore under his breath, noting that the Secret Service men were forced to separate. While Montgomery embraced Dara, in what Ridge was sure was a calculated move to provide a photo opportunity for the avid press, Ridge focused on the crowd.

"I can't tell you how much I appreciate all you've done," Montgomery said to Dara.

"I need to talk to you," Dara said, her voice fraying around the edges.

Montgomery hesitated, and out of the corner of his eye Ridge saw him give a reluctant nod. "I'll call you later," he promised.

The crowd grew more frenzied.

"Later," Ridge agreed, and firmly stuffed Dara into the car. Just as he rose, he heard the first shot, followed by shouts and screams of hysteria. Slamming the door closed, he saw an open space in front of Montgomery. His gut twisted, and he acted instinctively.

Ridge stepped in front of his father and took the bullet.

Thirteen

"**I** *am* family!" Dara yelled at the ER nurse.

Accustomed to dealing with hysteria, the nurse spoke in a low but firm voice. "Miss, I tried to explain. He's not out of surgery yet. As soon as he's in intensive care, you can see him."

Dara's tears welled in her eyes again. She felt so helpless. As soon as she'd seen Ridge go down, she'd scrambled out of the limo, despite shouted instructions to remain inside. "There was so much blood," she whispered, her mind tormenting her with the image of Ridge's too still body on the pavement.

"The bullet hit his spleen," the nurse explained, and motioned for an orderly. "He can take you to a quiet room," she said sympathetically, "where you can wait. Get her some coffee. She's Harrison Montgomery's goddaughter."

"Harrison's fine," she murmured. "Ridge may not be."
Hours passed, and she prayed. When Clarence arrived and

tried to get her to go home to change out of her blood-stained clothes, she refused.

"Harrison would insist—"

Dara's blood turned cold. "I don't want to hear about Harrison, right now." The man she loved was dying because he'd protected Harrison Montgomery. Her heart felt as if it had been wrenched from her chest. She gave in to the need to weep. Clarence awkwardly put his arm around her and patted her shoulder.

Finally the surgeon appeared in the doorway. "We removed his spleen," he told her. "He lost entirely too much blood, but this man must have something worth fighting for. I think he'll make it." He glanced at his watch. "He'll be in intensive care within fifteen minutes. The nurse says you're family?"

Dara sniffed and nodded. "We're going to be married."

Out of the corner of her eye she saw Clarence's jaw drop and she turned a challenging glare on him. "Isn't that right, Clarence?"

Blinking, Clarence cleared his throat. "Absolutely. Married," he repeated in dismay.

The strength returned to her legs and she ran to catch an elevator. It was twenty minutes instead of fifteen, and Dara was nearly climbing the wall when they wheeled Ridge's bed in. She bit her lip at the gray color of his skin. His lips were white, and he was so still that she wondered if the surgeon had made a mistake. The bleep of his monitor, however, indicated that his heart was beating.

For fifteen minutes of every hour, she sat and held his hand, alternating between words of love and softly uttered oaths that she would lock him up and throw away the key if he ever stepped in front of a bullet again.

Ridge awoke during one of her swearing sequences. He reached for her hand. "Dara."

Squeezing his cold fingers, Dara's eyes filled with tears. "Oh, Ridge. I love you so much, and you're going to be okay."

"I am?" he asked in an uncertain, slurred voice.

"Yes, oh, yes."

He frowned and swallowed with difficulty. His eyes closed. "Anybody else get hit?"

"No." Dara knew what he was asking. Her chest squeezed tight. "Nobody else got hit." She watched him drift off, and a peace settled over her. He would live.

The next time Ridge woke, he heard a man's voice. "I just want to thank you for saving my life," he said.

Ridge's heart raced. He tried to open his eyes, but his eyelids wouldn't cooperate. His mouth was as dry as sandpaper. "Montgomery?" he croaked.

"I owe you a debt that can't be repaid." Ridge heard the voice, but couldn't believe the words. He struggled for breath. Distantly, he heard a rapid beeping sound. "If I can ever do anything, anything at all—"

"Mr. Montgomery, you'll have to leave," a woman's voice said. "His monitors are going haywire."

Vainly licking his lips, Ridge heard another nurse murmur in agreement. He felt a comforting hand, but it wasn't Dara's, so he surrendered to sleep.

Anesthesia-induced dreams took him on a strange journey. Time and time again he saw himself stepping aside and letting Montgomery take the bullet. The sight of the older man dead on the pavement horrified Ridge. He tried to warn Montgomery, to yell, but his voice failed him.

Somewhere in the deepest, darkest part of him, an ugly voice reminded Ridge, *You wanted him dead.*

No!

You wanted him dead.

No! Ridge shook his head from side to side.

You wanted him dead.

I just wanted a father. "Oh, God, no."

"Stop, Ridge, please." Dara's pleading voice penetrated his nightmares. Cool hands soothed his forehead. "You've got to stop torturing yourself."

Ridge blinked. His vision was like a smudged lens, yet he knew it was her. His body warmed. His terror disappeared. "I love you," he managed in a husky voice, and began to see her more clearly.

Her eyes were filled with tears and love. She looked tired and wonderful. Tenderly touching his forehead, cheeks, and mouth, she bit her lip as she obviously tried to collect herself.

Ridge felt as if a terrible, crushing weight had been lifted from him, as if he'd been cured of an incurable disease. It took a moment before he realized exactly what it was. He stared at Dara in amazement. "I don't hate him anymore."

They were married within three weeks, and though Ridge preferred Tahiti, Dara insisted on a short flight time. They ended up on the island of St. John. He really couldn't complain, he thought as his wife brought him another fruity concoction from the well-stocked bar of their private beach cottage. He didn't mind watching her since she wore nearly nothing; a stretchy strapless top and a little skirt that made him wonder if she had anything on underneath it. She'd situated him on the large porch and threatened dire consequences if he moved.

The doorbell rang, and Dara quickly handed him the drink. "Don't you dare," she said when he swung his leg over the side of the lounger. "Just a minute," she murmured, and ran to sign for an express delivery letter. Carelessly tossing it on a teak end table, she joined him on the double chaise longue to watch the sunset.

Ridge lifted his arm around her shoulders and pulled her close. "You gonna tell me what's in that letter?"

She tangled her soft, smooth legs with his. "No. I'm going to seduce my husband." She pressed her lips behind his ear, and his blood pressure zoomed.

Gingerly, he turned on his side and kissed her long and luxuriously. Dara's eyes were hooded when he reluctantly pulled away for oxygen.

She sighed. "Since we can't make love on the beach this trip, I thought—"

"Why can't we?"

Dara hesitated. "Well, your injury, of course."

Ridge carefully pulled himself to his feet. "You know, you have this annoying habit."

Dara arched her eyebrows. "Another one?"

"I may not be ready to run a marathon, but I can handle a little nookie on the beach."

Dara sat up. "Ridge, I don't want you to hurt yourself."

Ridge slung a blanket over his shoulder. "Then we'll take a blanket. The sand can be a real bitch." He extended his hand to her, and when she shook her head mutinously, he sighed. "What's wrong?" he goaded her. "Are you chicken?"

Her eyes flashing, she flounced out of the chair. "If you end up in the hospital again..."

Ridge let her rant and rave a little more as he led her down the steps to the private beach. He knew *she* was still recovering from his being shot more than he was.

Ridge squeezed her hand and pulled her to him.

Dara's voice trailed off and her gaze locked with his.

He loosened her silky dark hair from its intricate braid, then unhooked her bandeau top to bare her breasts to the warm island breeze and his warmer gaze. He pressed his fingers to her lips and shook his head. "Sometimes it's hard to believe that it all worked out." He skimmed his hands down her neck to the swell of her breasts. "That you're mine."

Dara wrapped her arms around him and sighed. "Believe it."

Ridge was holding heaven. He nuzzled her forehead. "It would have been okay with me if you'd voted for your godfather on election day."

Dara shook her head. "He didn't need me. You did," she simply said, amazing him that her loyalties were so clearly drawn.

"I'll always need you," he told her. In the past few weeks he'd accepted his need for Dara, perhaps even welcomed it. He grinned slowly. "But I'm starting to wonder when my wife is going to seduce me on the beach."

Wearing a just-watch-me expression that had his libido screaming, she pulled the blanket off his shoulder and spread it over the white sand. Then she returned and kissed him with moist, blatantly sensual kisses until his blood drained to one aching part of his body. Her hands caressed his skin along with the breeze. Her nipples jutted enticingly against him. Sliding her fingers into the waistband of his shorts, she pushed them down. She wrapped her hand around his masculinity and gave a husky murmur of approval.

Ridge swallowed. "Why don't we take off your skirt?"

Dara dodged his hands, but continued to stroke him intimately. "Why don't you lay down on the blanket?"

Ridge groaned. He wasn't going to argue with her when she was stroking him into oblivion. Sucking in a deep breath, he stretched out on the blanket. A second passed and she was curling against him, her open mouth on his throat. Urgency whipped through him. "Honey, let's get rid of your skir—" Ridge broke off when his hands encountered not silk panties but the bare flesh of her derriere. "My oh, my," he muttered, and thanked heaven that his wife was adventurous. He shifted his hand and found her dewy and ready.

He toyed with her intimately until he heard the telltale hitch of her breath. She sank down on his aroused shaft, and they both sighed in satisfaction. Her hair shifted against his cheek, her eyes darkened with passion and love. His heart clenched almost painfully at the sight of her. She rode him gently to the soft rhythm of the lapping waves until they both cried out. The sunset faded, but the night and their life together had just begun.

The next morning Ridge woke to find Dara, clad in an oversize T-shirt, sitting cross-legged at the end of the bed facing him, reading some papers. Her eyebrows furrowed in concentration, she brushed her hair back from her face and shook her head. "Incredible," she murmured.

Ridge sat up. "What is?"

She glanced at him warily and hesitated. "Well, I'm not sure you're going to believe this," she said. "I'm not sure I believe it."

Her nerves were showing. Ridge frowned. "What?"

She avoided his gaze. "Guess I just better just start from the top," she said doubtfully.

"Right."

She took a deep breath and fiddled with the papers. "I hired a private detective to find out who that cowboy was in the tabloid picture, and he tracked the man down. So I got in touch with him. Well, his wife," she clarified. "Her name is Kelsey, and she didn't really want to talk to me until I started talking about Harrison and how he might have more than one illegitimate son, but I couldn't be sure . . ." Her voice trailed off and she bit her lip. "You're angry."

Ridge's head was spinning. "No." He shook his head. She'd surprised him such that he couldn't say what he was, but he definitely wasn't angry. "No," he repeated.

"But you haven't said anything."

"I haven't had a chance. What made you do this?"

"That night I caught you looking at his picture. Your face. You were suffering." Her face tightened in remembered pain. "It hurt to see you that way, so I decided to find out what I could and let you decide what you wanted to do."

Just like that. She saw that he was hurting and took care of it. Humbled by the depth of her love, Ridge pulled her closer. "You're amazing. You read my mind," he said roughly, and felt her sigh of relief. "What is his name?"

Dara's face softened. "Lucas. Lucas Caldwell. His mother knew Harrison in college."

His heart pounded. "You're saying I've got a half brother in Wyoming."

Dara nodded and took his hand. "And he wants to meet you."

It was almost too much for him to take in. One month ago he'd had no family, no one. Now he had Dara and a brother. And she had brought him his brother. "What do you know about him? What—"

She placed the papers in his lap. "Everything I know is in there." When he reached for the first sheet of paper, she stayed his hand. "But I think you should know that Kelsey Caldwell seems to think there might be another piece to this puzzle."

Epilogue

The other piece of the puzzle was Reese Marchand. The man was a reformed rogue who'd spent the past few years winning at Monte Carlo's high-roller tables. His mother had fallen in love with Harrison when he'd worked at the American embassy in Paris, thirty-six years ago, and Reese was the result of their affair.

Tall, dark and lean, Reese had a Cary Grant sophistication with a glimmer of James Dean recklessness. Dara suspected there'd been more than a hint of recklessness before he'd gotten married. The reason for his reformation was apparent. His wife, blond, beautiful, and very pregnant, Beth Langdon Marchand, was obviously the center of his life.

Dara stared at the assortment of people in the sunken den of her home and could scarcely believe it. They'd all come, and, based on how well the three men had gotten along this momentous February weekend, she suspected this was just the beginning of a new relationship between the sons of Harrison Montgomery. Warmth and acceptance permeated the group. Each man had found a compelling fulfillment through a woman. Though she'd always believed love made all kinds of things possible, Dara was amazed at the power of love and commitment in this situation.

With his wife Kelsey tucked snugly against his side, Lucas Caldwell, the eldest of the three men, sipped his after-dinner Amaretto and talked business with Ridge. Reese pulled a cue from the rack and eyed the antique billiards table with approval. "Anyone for a friendly game of billiards?" he invited, a subtle grin lifting his mouth.

Kelsey was the first to stand. She selected a cue and played her fingers over the wood. "Billiards is for sissies," she said, bold as her red hair. "Plus there's the fact that it's limited to three players. Let's play eight ball."

Temporarily speechless, Reese glanced at Lucas.

Dara watched Ridge stifle a chuckle. Lucas didn't bother. Grinning, he tossed his wife an admiring glance and took an unhurried stroll to the table. "I'm in," he said in his deceptively mellow voice. He would probably hang them all out to dry.

"I'm in, too," added Ridge, whom Dara suspected was curious to see yet another side of the men who shared half his parentage.

Reese dipped his head and winked with a player's charm. "Lady's choice, it is."

At first Dara had thought Lucas and Ridge were most similar; hardworking, intense, watchful. Reese told jokes and put everyone at ease. Last night, her husband, who was an expert at watching, corrected her. "Reese observes. He's smooth, though, uses that European charm, and people let down their guard. Watch how many times he asks Beth if she needs something tomorrow." Dara had lost count.

"I haven't played eight ball in a while," Beth began, clearly torn between joining the game and poring over the photo album in her lap. She glanced doubtfully at her rounded abdomen, then at Reese. Her lips tilted in a brilliant grin. "But I don't think I can tear myself away from these nude baby pictures of my husband."

Reese laughed, and as if he couldn't resist an opportunity to touch her, he slipped over to the sofa where she sat and kissed her. "The father of your child thanks you."

The love and affection in the room seemed to swell again. Like a tender embrace, Dara felt Ridge's warm gaze on her. "Are you joining us?" he asked.

Dara shook her head. "Not this time." She was so worried she was tempted to bite her French manicure down to the quick. It was all she could do not to glue herself to the window. Her stomach knotted.

Would he come?

Ridge watched her with the measuring gaze of a man who knew her inside out. "You don't want to beat the pants off your guests?" he asked.

Dara widened her eyes in mock innocence. "I thought you told me you don't want me showing my tricks to anyone but you."

Kelsey let out a whoop of approval. Lucas draped an arm around his wife and saluted Dara with his glass. "She has a point," Lucas said. "Is she any good?"

"Very," Ridge said, and let everyone wonder just what she was good at. Dara's cheeks heated. His expression said she hadn't fooled him and that he would expect an explanation later. A different woman might have found that threatening. Not Dara, because she knew that Ridge was just as determined to protect her happiness as she was his.

Dara told herself it would be okay if the new commander in chief showed, or if he didn't. During her numerous telephone conversations with Kelsey and Beth, she'd mentioned the possibility of arranging a visit with

Harrison. Surprisingly enough, for all their different backgrounds, the three sons shared a similar view of Harrison Montgomery. They didn't want a barbecue-on-the-White-House-lawn relationship with Harrison. They just wanted to meet him, face-to-face.

Dara's stomach twisted again. She glanced out the window and watched the snow continue to fall.

Would he come?

Could this visit ease a little of the pain Lucas, Reese, and especially important to her, Ridge, had experienced? Could it possibly happen tonight?

When Dara's housekeeper answered the door, her eyes widened. "Mr. Mont—" she began, and corrected herself. "Mr. President."

Despite the small pleasure Harrison Montgomery felt at his new title, he held up his leather-encased hand and shook his head. "Thank you. I'll announce myself," he told her. More than the winter snow chilled his bones tonight. It was, after all, a night of reckoning. A night of facing the choices of his past.

His press secretary, Drew Forrester, had strongly advised that Harrison cancel this meeting, but for once, Harrison bowed to fate and accepted that the time had come.

He felt more tense than when he had taken the oath of office. And even knowing what was yet to come, Harrison was still not prepared for the prospect of coming face-to-face with all he had sacrificed. Down the hall, the sound of laughter and a cue hitting the ball drew his attention to the sunken den.

His gut clenched in anticipation. Following the sound, he walked slowly toward the double doors, then forced himself to watch the scene behind the cut-glass windows. Three men and a woman were playing pool. Regret usurped even his guilt as his gaze latched onto the only offspring he would ever have, and yet, would never fully know.

His chest tightened, and Harrison remembered the women who'd borne those sons. His ambition always uppermost, he'd treated each of them callously. Donna Caldwell had been a youthful indiscretion. Remorse filtered past years of denial that he had ruined a sweet, naive young woman's life. Sylvie, the woman who'd captured his heart. He closed his eyes at the bittersweet memory of the woman he'd loved but not married. And Jenna Jackson had been young and passionate, a balm to his injured male pride. After his marriage to Helen, it was with Jenna that he'd indulged his anguish when Sylvie had found another man to marry.

Who would have known that Helen wouldn't bear children?

Filled with bitter grief, Harrison watched his three sons. Their brotherly camaraderie was apparent. They had overcome the circumstance of their births to become strong men. Despite Harrison's position and power, he realized he was nothing to his sons. He had missed the important events of their lives. He had missed too much. He fought the dark knowledge that beneath his golden, gleaming success lay a pit of personal failure.

According to the information Harrison had acquired about each son during the last month, Lucas would challenge his platform on ranchers' grazing rights. Challenge, Harrison thought, taking full measure of the tall, tough man, and possibly win. Reese, a successful French champagne executive, would charm the American wine industry, then leave them eating his dust. His heart tightened as his gaze fell on his youngest son. Ridge had saved his life and would claim the love and adoration of his goddaughter forever.

The warmth within the room beckoned, promising a thaw to the chill in his bones. Inexorably drawn to the scene, Harrison cracked open the door and stepped closer, hungry for something that had eluded him his whole life.

He heard a swift intake of breath, saw Dara's startled glance, and knew his private moment of introspection had passed. She quickly stood, knitting her fingers together.

"Ridge." Dara's voice trembled. "Reese. Lucas."

Harrison braced himself.

"There's someone who wants to meet you," Dara said as he stepped the rest of the way through the door.

Three dark heads lifted in his direction. He had never faced a more daunting moment in his life. The weight of his sons' collective gaze would surely be heavier than the national debt. He expected condemnation, perhaps even contempt. Instead, when he looked into their eyes, he saw peaceful self-acceptance and a formidable inner strength. And Harrison Montgomery was struck with the knowledge that a divine someone had taken his worst wrongs and made something right.

*   *   *   *   *

COMING NEXT MONTH

It's Silhouette Desire's 1000th birthday! Join us for a spectacular three-month celebration, starring your favorite authors and the hottest heroes of the decade!

#991 SADDLE UP—Mary Lynn Baxter

One night with Bridget Martin had cost April's *Man of the Month*, single dad Jeremiah Davis, his bachelorhood! But would his new bride be the perfect mom for his little girl?

#992 THE GROOM, I PRESUME?—Annette Broadrick

Daughters of Texas

Maribeth O'Brien was everything Chris Cochran wanted in a woman. So when she was left at the altar by her delinquent groom, Chris stepped in and said, "I do"!

#993 FATHER OF THE BRAT—Elizabeth Bevarly

From Here to Paternity

Maddy Garrett had never liked arrogant Carver Venner. But now he needed her help—and Maddy couldn't resist his adorable daughter…or the sexy single dad!

#994 A STRANGER IN TEXAS—Lass Small

One passionate encounter with a handsome stranger had left Jessica Channing one very pregnant woman. Now the mysterious man was back, determined to discover Jessica's secret!

#995 FORGOTTEN VOWS—Modean Moon

The Wedding Night

Although Edward Carlton claimed his lovely bride had left him on their wedding night, Jennie didn't remember her husband. But she'd do anything to discover the truth about her past—and her marriage….

#996 TWO WEDDINGS AND A BRIDE—Anne Eames

Debut Author

Brand-new bride Catherine Mason was furious when she caught her groom kissing her bridesmaid! So she went on her honeymoon with handsome Jake Alley—and hoped another wedding would soon be on the way….

MILLION DOLLAR SWEEPSTAKES

SILHOUETTE®

Desire®

Presents the conclusion of

SONS AND *Lovers*

COMING IN MARCH 1996

RIDGE: THE AVENGER by Leanne Banks

It was bad enough Ridge Jackson had been hired to protect feisty Dara Seabrook, now he was finding it impossible to resist the one woman who could never be his!

"For the best mini-series of the decade, tune into SONS AND LOVERS, a magnificent trilogy created by three of romance's most gifted talents."

—Harriet Klausner
Affaire de Coeur

Also Available:

SD #975 LUCAS: THE LONER—Cindy Gerard (1/96)
SD # 981 REESE: THE UNTAMED—Susan Connell (2/96)

As seen on TV!
Free Gift Offer

With a Free Gift proof-of-purchase from any Silhouette® book,
you can receive a beautiful cubic zirconia pendant.

This gorgeous marquise-shaped stone is a genuine cubic
zirconia—accented by an 18" gold tone necklace.

(Approximate retail value $19.95)

Send for yours today…
compliments of ▼ *Silhouette*®
TM

To receive your free gift, a cubic zirconia pendant, send us one original proof-of-purchase, photocopies not accepted, from the back of any Silhouette Romance™, Silhouette Desire®, Silhouette Special Edition®, Silhouette Intimate Moments® or Silhouette Shadows™ title available in February, March or April at your favorite retail outlet, together with the Free Gift Certificate, plus a check or money order for $1.75 U.S./$2.25 CAN. (do not send cash) to cover postage and handling, payable to Silhouette Free Gift Offer. We will send you the specified gift. Allow 6 to 8 weeks for delivery. Offer good until April 30, 1996 or while quantities last. Offer valid in the U.S. and Canada only.

Free Gift Certificate

Name: _____

Address: _____

City: _____ State/Province: _____ Zip/Postal Code: _____

Mail this certificate, one proof-of-purchase and a check or money order for postage and handling to: SILHOUETTE FREE GIFT OFFER 1996. In the U.S.: 3010 Walden Avenue, P.O. Box 9057, Buffalo NY 14269-9057. In Canada: P.O. Box 622, Fort Erie,

---

FREE GIFT OFFER   079-KBZ-R
ONE PROOF-OF-PURCHASE
To collect your fabulous FREE GIFT, a cubic zirconia pendant, you must include this
original proof-of-purchase for each gift with the properly completed Free Gift Certificate.

079-KBZ-R

You're About to Become a *Privileged Woman*

Reap the rewards of fabulous free gifts and benefits with proofs-of-purchase from Silhouette and Harlequin books

Pages & Privileges™

It's our way of thanking you for buying our books at your favorite retail stores.

Harlequin and Silhouette—
the most privileged readers in the world!

For more information about Harlequin and Silhouette's PAGES & PRIVILEGES program call the Pages & Privileges Benefits Desk: 1-503-794-2499

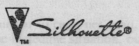